the wolf that rode

The Wolf That Rode

by

NELSON NYE

New York

THE MACMILLAN COMPANY

1960

First Printing

The Macmillan Company, New York
Brett-Macmillan Ltd., Galt, Ontario

Printed in the United States of America

Library of Congress catalog card number: 60–7283

the wolf that rode

1

ALTHEA was a lavender blaze in the sun, the burro weeds still dustily green, when Brett Fasken came out of the cedar brakes and got his first look in six years at those dun and red bluffs stacked like daubed cardboard behind Packer's Crossing.

Country looked dry—powerful dry, he thought, eying it; the San Pedro little more than a guttering gurgle scarce reaching the hocks of the flax-tailed chocolate roan he was forking. He'd never seen the river so low or the roundabout range so God-awful yellow at this time of year. But it was good to be back. He hoped it was anyhow.

A dozen familiar things caught his notice as he sat with a knee carelessly crooked about the horn of his heavy stock saddle, nostalgically packing his short stubby pipe. Over there was that thicket where he'd shot his first gobbler—he'd been ten at the time and so swelled up with pride the crew had taken to calling him 'Dead Eye.' Yonder, by the bend and half hidden in the heat-cured fronds of yellowing salt cedar, was where he'd dropped the twenty-point buck.

He grinned, remembering Jo's disgust at having to come all this way from the ranch to cut up a bothersome nuisance's kill. Jo—short for Josephine—was Brett's notionable sister, older by six years and, even in those days, no one to thumb your nose and yell boo! at. Belle of every party, she had drawn men like flies. Maybe, Brett mused, that had been her real trouble, having things too easy and never being wrong. A man once in a while liked to be right himself.

Brett sighed. He'd sighed a-plenty over Jo. She'd got everything she wanted, barring one. If a man could put any stock in rumor she'd never got a ring. The feller she'd been real set on—Clint Wilder—had gone and got himself killed. It had fallen on Brett to tell her Clint wasn't coming back ever. He could recall in dreary detail each hour of the night which had finally decided him to quit this damned country. Jo'd done her best after the Old Man died to make something of Brett—you had to give her that. He'd been stubborn as a Neuches steer, wanting to make his own mind up. And he had by God done it!

He'd never regretted signing over his share of the ranch. The sap had been coming up in him then; he wasn't taking nobody's word for what he might find beyond the rim of the next hill. In six years he'd seen for himself. Right now he wouldn't have traded that experience for a dozen ranches of the kind Hobbled O had become.

Scratching a match he puffed, considering.

Wouldn't be any welcome mats out. As a kid there had always been a chip on Brett's shoulder and he'd been eternally into something. These were the things this town would remember. He'd have to make a place for himself, and—no getting around it—he'd have trouble with Jo.

She was touchy—inclined, as Brett saw it, to put too high a value on appearances and standing, and on the powerful position she'd made for Hobbled O in particular. Such things never bothered Brett; she could have her fat place in this puddle—could be Queen of the May for all he cared.

He had a hunch she wouldn't believe that. Be like kicking a sore-backed bull in the butt, him coming back here. Jo was strong on logic—the female kind. She liked decorum and due process, especially in others. She liked to be kowtowed to and there wasn't a kowtowing bone in Brett's body. And if there was any one thing she *couldn't* abide it would be change—the merest hint of any change that might be brought about by others.

He puffed some more. "God damn it," he said, "I got a right to put down roots here!" He was tired, fed up with roving; there came a time when a man wanted something better, when the pleasures of former times no longer pleased. There was nothing wrong with being a roughneck but there was a point of no return and a range bum at forty was a sure as hell sorry sight!

That he lacked several years of reaching forty made no difference; it was near enough. Maybe he didn't have to shove himself right under her nose—there were plenty other places where a man could start over, where he wouldn't be half buried under all the things that couldn't be undone. But this, right here, was where it had started. This was the town that had given him the bad name, that had put the mad dog tag on him. He'd got a heap to live down; if there was ever to be any redemption for Brett Fasken he would have to look for it here.

Coming back hadn't been any spur-of-the moment impulse; a lot of sleepless nights had gone into the decision. He had reckoned it wouldn't be easy and the closer he came the more impossible it looked. But if a man truly wanted to put the past behind there was only one place on God's earth he could do it. For Brett that place was Packer's Crossing.

He was a dark-haired man, big-shouldered, broad of chest with sun-darkened cheeks and a wind-ruddied face etched with the marks of past dangers. One ear was thickened to more than twice its proper size. His nose was a humpbacked hook too many fists had tampered with. A scar ran from his left eyebrow well into the hairline and two of his front teeth were mostly gold. He limped —not too badly yet observedly.

As he approached the town he noted that it hadn't changed a great deal. It still looked like something that had been fished through a knothole, the clapboard sheathings more grayly weathered, the adobes showing more cracks, less plaster. Wind still blew yellow dust through its streets. The original settlement, staked out around the ford, was now completely abandoned. Current business was carried on at a higher level in the hodgepodge of buildings strewn along the old Butterfield trail a mile and a half west and some three hundred feet higher where a breath of air might conceivably be trapped.

There was a bakeshop now and a window of women's hats which was new to him; and the wind, as Brett remembered it, had never been so hot. It had the scorched earth smell of Death Valley.

The old Red Wall was still selling nourishment. The dock of Joe Able's Mercantile appeared stacked with more incoming goods than Brett could recall ever before having noticed; but none of these places looked as big as he remembered.

McInery evidently still ran the livery. Brett thought back with a sheepish grin to the fight he'd staged with a visiting pugilist on the old Scot's manure pile when he'd knocked that fool bruiser clean through the back wall. McInery would remember that—he'd been all of a week rounding up escaped horses. Schrader, at the Red Wall, likely wouldn't have forgot Brett either. Jo was the one that would really be fussed though. Jo would work at it.

Brett got down before the Mercantile, loosely knotting the reins. He guessed Jo was just going to have to get used to it. God, but that sun was hot!

He backhanded a surplus of sweat off his cheeks, and felt the rubbery rasp of beard stubble. Glancing around as he moved up the steps, he halted a moment in the trapped heat of the porch to watch a dappling of sunlight and shadow that wind and a ragged tuft of cloud were hustling up the wagon-cluttered street. Shaking his head he reached out for the door.

His hand ran into something yielding that crackled and abruptly dropped away in a series of miniature explosions of sound that whipped Brett about as though a rope had laid hold of him.

All he saw right away was her dark stormy eyes, blue flashes like silver ripping through a summer night. Then his stare took in her mop of yellow hair, her angry mouth, the curves below it.

Welcome to Friedman Branch Library!
You checked out the following items:

1. The stars are fire : a novel
   Barcode: 31019005638401 Due:
   09/06/2017 11:59 PM
2. The wolf that rode
   Barcode: 31057901790355 Due:
   09/14/2017 11:59 PM
3. Hillbilly elegy : a memoir of a
   family and culture in crisis
   Barcode: 31019005565299 Due:
   09/14/2017 11:59 PM

ARCPLS-FRMAN 2017-08-30 17:33
You were helped by Danica

1000 Books Before Kindergarten
Register Today!

He dragged off his hat and shifted his eyes uncomfortably to the profusion of parcels tumbled over the dusty boards. The quiet cotton of betrayed 'unmentionables' protruded from one burst wrapping. He swallowed, embarrassed by her crimson blush, stepped involuntarily back, hastily disengaging his glance.

"Why don't you watch where—" She stopped, mouth open, eyes sprung wide as, inside the store, someone incredulously gasped: "Brett Fasken!"

The color thinned from her cheeks, and an unfathomable expression came into her stare.

"Sorry, ma'am," Brett muttered. He stooped and commenced gathering her bundles, feeling about as prominent as a tenderfoot trapper skinning his first skunk. The spilled drawers—that's what they sure enough were—he got hold of like he would a live snake, grimly, trying to squash them back out of sight and making mean work of it.

He stood up, jaws red as fire, and gave her another parched look as he straightened. "I'll tote 'em," he growled.

She had hold of herself now, the whole look of her more guarded. The quickness of her mind was apparent when she said, "Lola Trone," abruptly. "I wasn't around when you—left." Her eyes dug at him more insistently. "Are you Brett *Fasken?*"

Brett's cheeks turned perceptibly darker. Curiously reluctant for a man who'd never cared what others thought, he nodded. There was an implied need, almost an urgency, in her tone he could not help but notice. "Expect I'll have to plead guilty," he said. "Where-at's your rig?"

Her eyes continued to hold him. Simultaneously both of them became aware of the dragged-out silence. "Right over there —" her words tumbled over each other, "in front of the bakeshop." She took a deep breath. "You needn't trouble. I can manage."

"Pleasure," Brett said, ignoring her hands. He stepped aside to let her pass, seeing the faces pull back from the windows.

He considered the swing of her hip and shoulder as he trailed her around a tangle of wagons to a dilapidated buggy and stowed her parcels in the space behind the seat. There was no top to the thing, and its wood looked gray as the store porch steps.

She stood darkly watching. "I suppose you're here to claim your part of the estate."

"Come again?" Brett said.

"Hobbled O."

The way she said it made a curse of the name. Brett's eyes considered her cool, set face. The heat in this bright saffron light hardly touched her. She had smooth skin tanned deeply enough to give her a kind of half-gypsy look. Her age he put at a probable twenty.

"I can see you haven't much use for the outfit."

"As a part of what your sister calls 'trash,' about average, I'd say."

This seemed like to be a heap worse than he'd figured. He blew sweat off his nose. "You're a small owner then?"

"My brother," she said flatly, "runs Scab 8—on the Aravaipa."

He peered at her curiously. What the hell ailed her? What was happening around here? She'd heard the stories, of course, but what was Jo up to that could put this dark look on her, that could turn this girl so apprehensively hostile?

The girl's eyes continued to pry and dig at him as though she were trying to run something down, something black and ugly that she was obviously afraid of. He'd seen that look on cowtown marshals getting ready to tell him he had better shove on.

He tried a smile. "I expect I'm supposed to know what you're drivin' at—"

"Didn't Mister Joseph send for you?"

Brett had heard they were calling his sister that. According to the talk he'd picked up here and there she already claimed about two-thirds of this country and had her sights set toward gobbling the rest of it. This might even be true; it sounded enough like her. But the idea of Josephine sending for *him* was farfetched enough to make Brett Fasken laugh.

The girl's eyes blazed.

"It's plain," Brett said, sobering, "you don't know Jo very well."

"Then why did you come back!"

It wasn't the words, it was her tone that angered him. He said more harshly than perhaps he should have, "Any law against it?"

She got into the buggy, ignoring his hand.

Brett smothered his annoyance. "She after your place?"

"She's trying to make my brother out a rustler!"

2

BRETT stood at the bar in the Red Wall saloon before an untasted whisky, still thinking about Lola Trone. The apron was new to him, nor did he place any of the faces in this room as old acquaintances; he was oddly troubled about this, remembering Schrader's place as the principal hang-out for roistering cowhands. Seemed like even on an off day, spang in the middle of it, there ought to be something going on here.

A dealer at one of the empty back tables kept shuffling and reshuffling an unused deck of freshly broken-out cards. The five low-talkers with their heads together farther down the bar had the patched-together hardscrabble look of greasy-sackers; beyond the original desultory interest any range tramp might have attracted, they'd ignored him—not that he gave a damn. It was just queer, like the glimpse he had caught of Ollie Schultz in the mirror coming up to the batwings and then sheering away like the heel flies was after him.

Idly considering the men in the glass he reflected you could mighty near always pick out a small owner by the sullen half-defiant, almost furtive scrinch of his stare. They seemed eternally to need justification, as though the world owed them something it was trying to get out of. Take a middlin'-to-fair self-respecting cowpoke and give him enough to get a start of his own and right away he got that look on him, like he was packing a chip and half scared, half wanting, somebody to put a hand on it.

Ollie had started as a Hobbled O puncher. Then he'd got in the way of a big cow during roundup. He'd been handling the

8

iron and had got an arm gored. After they'd taken it off the Old Man had set him up at a line camp and given him the place when he'd saved up enough to buy some cows of his own. You'd think there'd be some loyalty in him, but being on his own had put a flea in his bonnet. He'd fenced off the water up there and gone to patrolling it with a gun. Most big owners would have plowed him under, but the Old Man had passed it off with a laugh. Now the Old Man was dead and with Mister Joseph running things Brett couldn't help but wonder what had happened to that place.

No paper had changed hands; the Old Man would have been insulted if anyone had ever talked paper at him. He'd been a man of his word and expected others to be. Come right down to it there was mighty little paper anywhere in this country. This was a free grass region; all anyone had actual claim to was a few home-place acres and whatever else he was able to make stick.

Brett scowled moodily. This San Pedro country was a long ride from the Great White Father. Took a hardy breed to settle a back of beyond. That kind of people got in the habit of making their own rules; to survive they just about had to. They wouldn't cotton to bunch quitters and yet, paradoxically, it was a community of loners, each a free thinker bitterly resenting any suggestion of restraint. There weren't any resident judges and courts were for the feeble-minded, the final resort of weaklings the country would be better off without. That girl had sure given Brett something to think about.

This was still a gun-wearing country. Brett knew how obdurate Jo could be—stubborn as any mule! That business of Clint had hit her hard; hard enough, maybe, to turn her mean as what little he'd heard had painted her. She always had been inclined to push. She hadn't ever been devious that Brett could remember, and if she took Trone for a cow thief the chances were he probably was. If Jo wanted Trone's place she was big enough to take it—wasn't she?

She'd got big all right, but that very fact could be working against her. With a sister pretty as this girl Brett had talked to Trone might have most of these free-grassers back of him; and you had to remember how much importance Jo attached to the weight of public opinion. She'd have to seem within her rights; she'd want that much justification. She'd know exactly how far she could fly in the face of providence. There might be political fences. She would want to look well to outsiders. She was a woman who'd always put a heap of stock in standing, an aristocrat born out of her time. She'd made Hobbled O known all over Arizona; she'd be on eye-rolling terms with the Governor and all the rest of the big moguls. Thing like that could cramp your style. Maybe she'd been told to take it a little slow.

Brett went out of the place without touching his drink. He'd reckoned to be looked at some askance, but he sure hadn't figured to be walking into a squabble that branded him before he ever opened his mouth.

The Mercantile when he stepped into it had just about everything in sight but customers. Jack Able, getting up from a lunch at the cracker barrel, more resembled a crane than he ever had but Yukon ice wouldn't have been more chilly.

"Johnny, get your gun," the man said, still with that fishy look on his cheeks as a pimply-chinned youngster came in from the back tying the strings of a hastily-got-into apron. The boy, throwing Brett a startled glance, hared off. Brett eyed the merchant sternly, but reckoned nothing he could say was like to make things more favorable. Brett Fasken, to those who'd remember him, spelled Trouble. "The bad penny," he said, nodding. "Jack, how are you?"

Able made no move to put out a paw. "You must of come from the back end of China."

"Near enough." Brett could feel the man's dislike and suspicion. "I'd like a couple lengths of your heaviest cotton rope."

"Got the money to pay for 'em?"

Brett dropped a silver dollar on the counter. Able, sourly

grunting, tramped off through a dangling of long-handled underwear. "About that rope?" Brett said when he came back.

"I ain't no mind reader. What lengths you want?"

"Figure to work one of them into a halter shank. About
twenty foot'll do for the other." Glancing around, Brett said, "You
been laying in for a rush or somethin'?"

The storekeeper wheeled away without talk. Coming back
with the rope he looked about as sociable as an ulcerated tooth.
"Man can't make no livin' eatin' the stuff off his shelves!"

"Jo?" Brett said. "Thought you and her was *buen amigos*."

"We git along," said Able shortly. He picked up Brett's cart-
wheel and skinned it into a drawer. "Come to a dollar five," he
growled.

Brett put down another nickel and said, "That Trone girl
working for Hobbled O, is she?"

Able said resentfully, "Long's they've got the cash t' pay with
I don't figure t' turn 'em away— Go tell Jo that if you've a mind
to!"

Brett said after a moment, "How's Hobbled O getting along
with Currycomb?" Currycomb, from what he'd heard, was the
only other big neighbor left.

"They're still speakin'."

"How about the little fellers?"

"If you don't know what's goin' on," Able snarled, "you
better find out about it someplace else!"

While Brett was eying him the porch boards thumped and
boomed to booted feet. Syd Stoker came in, his beefy shoulders
trailed by the tight-skinned face of Ollie Schultz.

Brett nodded to the pair. The town's tin still glinted on
Stoker's sun-greened vest. He was a big man and run to fat, but
there'd been a time, Brett remembered, when Syd had been a
man you'd better step around with care.

"So you've come back," the marshal said. "Josephine send for
you?"

"Oh, for God's sake!" Brett cried, exasperated, "Why in hell would Jo send for *me?*"

"I'd expect you to know better about that than us, but I could scrape up a couple of reasons if I was pushed hard."

Schultz—gaunt, wire-drawn with the sprung legs of a veteran cowhand and the ass-pinched look of a badgered nester—appeared to have no patience for beating around the bush. There was fright in his eyes and, far back, a desperation nearly hidden behind his outrage.

Brett thought of that cow camp his father had given Schultz, tucked away up there among the hoot owls and eagles in the hidden and rocky ramparts of the Glory Mountains back of Hobbled O. Schultz was a man who had married late in life and taken a mail-order bride to his bed. One-armed and defying the code of the range, he had cause to look wild if he still had that place. The man was a bunch quitter, a renegade in the eyes of the brand that had fed him—in the eyes of this whole country, so far as that went. They might not like Jo but what Schultz had done was an offense against all of them. He'd been living quite a while on borrowed time by the look of him.

Brett's eyes slid around to the marshal but there was nothing written on Stoker's face. Brett's own cheeks drew in a bit at the creases. He saw a number of things he might better have done than come back to this range where his name was just something people used to relieve themselves.

His shoulders stirred. He said to Schultz mildly, "Bug get stuck in your craw, Ollie?"

Openly shaking in the grip of his emotions, the man glared as though Brett had bedded his wife. "I tell you this," Schultz said hoarsely—"don't come py mine blace! You keep outa dem beaks or, py Gott, you ged kilt!"

3

SCHULTZ rushed from the store with a great wheezing breath like a sob tearing out of him. All this embarrassed Brett; the quality of the stillness began to rise like walls about him.

The marshal said, "He meant that, Fasken."

"Jesus Christ!" Brett cried, feeling boxed. "Has a man got to account for every fart that gets loose!"

Able's eyes were like gimlets. "If you got nothin' to hide why don't you say why you're here then?"

"You got a wild hair, too?"

Stoker said heavily, "We got enough trouble around here now. This whole country's crouched on black powder. Might clear the air if you'd declare yourself." Shifting his weight, he appeared to reach a decision. "Maybe you'd better just get on your horse and—ah—drop back into whatever you left to come over here."

"You making that an order, Syd?"

"Somebody kills that boneheaded Dutchman you could find yourself without a leg to stand on." Stoker irritably pushed a hand through the air. "Wouldn't look very good if he should happen all of a sudden to turn up missing."

Brett scowled, sighing. "I've got nothing to do with the troubles of—" But even while he was speaking he could see this might not be entirely true, for who could say how far back this went? Quite as much of the responsibility for Stoker's dark imaginings might belong to him as could be charged against Jo. Come right down to it this might all stem from Brett. Clint Wilder

13

came into his head and he stood silent, somberly staring at nothing.

"If you didn't come here with nothing special on your mind—" Stoker began.

"I came back to start over."

The storekeeper's jaw dropped. His false teeth clicked together and he uttered a disbelieving snort.

"Well," Stoker said, not quite looking at Brett, "there's a heap of other places—"

"This is where I belong."

Able began, "You didn't figure that way—"

"A man's values change. Six years ago, Joe, you was unloadin' flour at ten dollars a barrel."

Able's stare went over Brett's brush-ripped clothes and all his testiness appeared to boil up again. The marshal said, "Wait —" putting out a hand. His stare dug into Brett. "How much do you figure that half-interest's worth?"

Brett looked at him. "It ain't worth a thing without a man has got it. That place belongs to Jo."

Able made a loud noise. "All who believe that can stand on their head!"

The marshal said to Brett, "That's pretty hard to swallow— even knowin' your sister. The Old Man would have—"

"Sure. He did. But I signed it all over to Jo."

"I don't believe it!" Able snarled.

Brett's cheeks thinned but he let the words pass.

Stoker said, "Couple of fellers seem to've come up with the notion your sister's about set to take over this country. Been a pile of cartridges laid in this past month. You showin' up ain't—"

"I can't help that."

"Nobody settin' on your shirttail. Ain't like you had to do this right now," the marshal finished.

Brett was tempted. Why not? he asked himself, as he had

done a dozen times. But he knew if he didn't stay now he never would. He'd just keep drifting, sliding on down the ladder, taking the course of least resistance. Running, same as drinking, got to be a powerful habit.

He looked at them tiredly. He felt sorry for Stoker; the marshal was getting along to where the old days were something he had to remember. When a man got into his fifties there was no percentage packing a gun. You could see it in Stoker. You could see that he knew it. You could see what that knowledge was doing to him, too.

Brett shook his head. "It took me six years to get enough sense to come back here. I don't like this deal any better than you but I got to stick, Syd. Run now and I'll be runnin' the rest of my life."

"You stay," Able sneered, "an' that may not be long."

Stoker said, "Everybody knows your old man left you half of that place."

Brett eyed the marshal with exasperation. "Told you I give my half to Jo. Don't take my word for it; go look up the records."

"There's been no change. You're down as half owner."

Brett's mouth tightened. "Jo can clear that up."

"Can, maybe, but will she? Over the years," Stoker said with a dust-dry care, "your sister could've done a great plenty if she'd been minded to. I'm not one to demean her. I'll give credit where it's due; she's built Hobbled O to where no spread in this country —exceptin' Currycomb, maybe—could get near enough to touch it with a ten-foot pole. *How* she's done it is something else again. We don't want to see no more of that."

Brett said thinly, "You accusin' her of rustlin'?"

He saw the storekeeper grin.

"There's other ways to build a spread. Ways that the law can't put its fingers on. Sheriff knows what's going on," Stoker said. "He's keepin' plumb out of it. But that don't make it right.

I'm goin' to tell you this: Them that's standin' against her now is just as bull-stubborn as she is. They've give all they're goin' to. You better see that she knows that."

Brett could feel this thing closing in on him. He thought of all the places his fiddle feet had taken him. Not one of them was home. None had put the brand on him. All they'd done was make it plainer. Drifting hadn't solved anything.

He said finally, "If you think it will do any good I'll talk to her, but I'm not pulling out."

"What *are* you gonna do?" Able said, eying him slanchways.

"I'm going to get me a job if I can latch onto one."

"Think anyone would hire Brett Fasken round here?" Able said, ignoring the marshal's warning glance, "I'd as soon pick up a sidewinder an' shove it in my pocket."

Brett took that, too. He had known this wouldn't be easy.

"Drought has hit them all," Stoker said. "They're all on credit, either to Able or your sister."

"Currycomb?"

"Well—" Stoker said, "I guess Currycomb can weather it. You reckon they'd hire you?"

"Must have some horse stock they'd like to get broke."

"They've got men to handle that."

"I'm willin' to work on shares," Brett told them. "What about this feller, Trone?"

The marshal thought a long while before he said, "What about him?"

Brett wasn't quite sure why he had brought Trone into this but it looked like it had been a poor thing to do. He couldn't think of any way to get himself off the hook. He said, "I talked with his sister. You sure this Trone's honest?"

The marshal peered at him, affronted, and said, "How did you happen to be talking to Trone's sister?"

Brett told him, adding, "She seemed to think Jo was trying—"

"I don't want to hear any more about it."

"Trouble," Brett said, "is best dragged out in the open where a man—"

Stoker wheeled about and stalked off.

Brett, listening to the marshal's boots thump down the steps, looked hard at Able.

"Mebbe Trone will put you on," Able said—"why don't you go out there?" When Brett continued silently to watch him Able said, half snorting: "You better git yourself a sixshooter an' have it where you can git at it!"

Brett understood that he had overstayed his welcome. "What's that supposed to mean?" he said, but Able didn't back off this time. He stood his ground with a look of relish.

"Mister Joseph has called a meetin' for tonight, a full-dress powwow of the local association. They're fixin' to outlaw Trone an' rule him off this range. An' here's somethin' more you can smoke in that pipe. Stoker thinks the sun rises an' sets in that girl. An' the first time he steps outa line your big mogul sister'll have that badge off his vest. Pretty, ain't it?" he grinned, rubbing his hands. "That's what you've stepped into, Fasken, an' I hope the goddam hell it chokes you!"

4

BRETT strode unseeingly into the stifling glare, less concerned with where his feet might take him than with his whirling thoughts. "Jo—Jo!" he groaned, cursing Clint Wilder as he never had before.

He tried to walk it off, to convince himself this was fool kid crazy; knowing even as he tramped that he was caught in it now. No man could hide from the things that ailed him. As a stone dropped into a quiet pool throws out rings in ever-widening circles, so the facts of a life—the hidden facets of one's past—keep reaching out with groping fingers until all the trembling threads of the present, those good intentions, actual achievements, are ripped to tatters and count for no more than ashes dropped in a privy.

It was a cruel knowledge, a burden no man should be asked to bear—had he come all these weary miles for this? Was nothing better possible? Were a man's past shortcomings to hound him forever? Or was there hope, some real salvation, in the compulsion, the inexplicable urges, that had dragged him back to face up to that past?

He'd no remembrance of where he had been or what he had done or seen or heard when, at close on to four, he found himself in front of the bank, staring at the shape of himself in the glass. Those broad restless shoulders, the hard bulges of muscle, the scraggle of bristle that darkened his jaws—that disreputable hat. Brett Fasken!

How in God's name had he gotten to this!

He wheeled away, blackly cursing.

He hadn't touched whisky for months but now, abruptly, every parched inch of his body cried out. He broke into a stumbling run and pushed blindly through the Red Wall's batwings.

The place was filled, packed and crowded and suddenly still. Any other time that stillness would have hauled him out of his shell. He pushed through the men, unnoticing, bellying up to the bar, pounding the wood with his fists, growling: "Whisky!"

Ben Schrader came up in his plug hat, eyes watchful. "Heard you was back." He said, plain and careful, "I don't want no trouble."

Brett's glance took him in. "You goin' to stand there all night?" He pawed four bits out of a pocket, slapped it down.

"You look like you've had enough now," Schrader mumbled.

"Just put out the bottle."

Schrader was minded to refuse and too obviously unsettled by thoughts of what might follow. Brett's stare turned mocking. "Damned if you don't an' maybe if you do." Impatience rasped through the show of his teeth. "I don't give a rip which but make it quick."

Schrader pushed out a bottle, the progress of it loud in this unnatural quiet. At either side of Brett men eased away, trying not to be noticed. Brett, approving the label, paid them no attention. He was reaching for the bottle when the batwings skreaked and someone came across the room at a walk.

"Your name Fasken?"

The man was slim, a reedy youth with a too-bright stare, garbed in a store-bought suit of flashy check. He was handsome in a weak immaturish way and carried himself with considerably more confidence than Brett could see any reason for.

Brett, watching him in the glass, thought *Here we go!* and settled all the weight of his arms on his elbows. The West had a deal too many of this kind. Every train from the East was spewing them forth at the rail ends as though this was the only export specimen it produced. They came in all sizes and shapes, he thought sourly—self-satisfied, cocky as feisty pups: bright young men bound to make their marks, bringing civilization to these far frontiers.

"Go away," he said without bothering to turn.

He saw the hate and anger piling into the man's stare and casually came around as the fellow started to reach for him. "I wouldn't," Brett said.

"I asked you a question!"

"You did?" Brett said.

The young man's cheeks got nearly red as the curled hair cut in exaggerated burnsides beneath the cant of his impeccable brown derby.

Brett looked mildly amused. "You ain't packin' no tin. You got a God-given right?"

The place became so still there was no describing it. The young fellow's expression, for a moment, appeared almost ludicrous. "Careful," Brett drawled, "you'll bust your surcingle."

The kid whipped up his fist but Brett slid around it, throwing a cuff of his own to the jaw. It was like hitting a quarter of beef with a board. The derby flew off and bounded over the floor. The young man, both arms flapping, stumbled backward and sat down.

A lock of red hair dangled over one eye giving him a kind of startled elfin look that most times would have drawn ribald comment. The crowd stood like cattle frozen into their tracks, and baffled, drink forgotten, Brett was wheeling away to get out of the place when a sharp intake of breath spun him into a wide-eyed crouch. The fellow he'd struck had a pawing hand buried to the wrist in his coat.

Brett, acting on instinct, lunged forward with a roar. If it was a gun the kid had been fixing to lay hold of, Brett's shout so flustered him he got it caught in the lining. Brett's flying leap took him near enough to upset the fellow again, spilling him in a roll and sending him bounding after that forest of retreating legs.

No one laughed. Every face Brett's glance encountered

showed a kind of crawling horror. He went after the kid, yanking him upright and holding him there by a fistful of coat with his dangling boots barely making contact with the floor.

The kid didn't look so dapper with that sawdust all over him and the hair hanging down like a mop in his face and the whites of his eyes peering groggily through it.

Brett shifted his grip, half minded to shake him. He thrust his free hand inside the checked coat and found the snagged pistol, ripping it loose and sending it backhanded in revolving flight through the glass of a window. The crash and the fellow's ragged breathing were isolated sounds in the still, packed room.

The brittle quiet angered Brett almost as much as the rest of it. All he'd asked was the chance to show these fools he wasn't the kind they had tabbed him for, and all he had done—but there was more to it than this. Just confirming their beliefs wouldn't have put that look on them. This bunch was scared green, and not of him—that much he sensed. Every frantic eye was fixed on the kid.

"You don't look like much to me," Brett said, and spun him around, grabbing hold of his collar. With his free hand catching up the slack of the kid's pants Brett ran him a few feet to get him started and let go. The kid went like a heaved rock through the batwings.

Brett looked at the crowd. You'd have thought, by God, he had smallpox or something.

A scrabbling, a muttering, a stagger of boot sound, came through the open windows. A pony crow-hopped, snorting. Leather squealed. Hoofs stamped hollowly across the groan of planks and the front of a horse abruptly parted the doors. Sunlight, gushing in around it, sped over the floor and up men's legs. "You in there, Fasken! Next time we meet be heeled, goddam you!"

Booting back one of the doors the kid whirled his horse with a brutal rein and was gone in a climbing thunder of hoofs.

"Cheap an' loud." Brett turned back to the bar, no longer

wanting his drink but not wanting either to give this bunch the satisfaction of thinking they had made it too uncomfortable for him.

There was still no talk, not even from Schrader who was eying the broken slats of the door. There was a sudden sound of boots and Syd Stoker, the marshal, shoved in looking grim. "What's the matter with the kid?"

Brett turned around. "He needed a lesson. I give it to him."

There were a lot of things the marshal might have said and some of them Brett was halfway expecting, but Stoker handled this different. "You know who that was?"

Brett, with his look showing he didn't give a damn, turned once more to pick up his whisky.

"That was Rhode Island Red."

"Never heard of him," Brett said, and tossed off his drink.

"You will," Stoker growled. "Do this town a favor and get out of here, will you?"

The feel of the place was bad and getting worse. It kept plucking Brett's nerve ends like a hitch at his sleeve. Putting his glass on the bar, he said, "I guess not." He thought of the warning that cheap john had given him. He put a coin beside the glass, turning to consider the plowed-up face of the marshal. "Who is this pecker-neck, anyway?"

Stoker locked eyes with him. "About the killin'est varmint that's hit these parts. Four men in three years—that much I can tell you. Shot them down just like dogs, never movin' a hand till he'd prodded 'em into reachin'. Fennison, Biltkey, Drucks, an' Ryan," he said, ticking them off on his fingers, every one of them owners if you counted greasysackers. "Better take my advice. That feller can remember clean back to the Ark."

He walked over and picked up the kid's dented derby. Absently brushing its nap he fetched his glance around. "You'd have no more show than a stump-tailed bull in fly-time."

"Never expected to find you worryin' about me."

Stoker said, snorting, "You better know this—if you don't already. It ain't only he's fast. Shadow of your sister hangs over that kid. He lives in the house an' nobody—not even Bill Tice—sets out to tell him what to do."

"I don't think," Brett began, but the marshal cut through.

"Think what you want. Just take it from me that feller can't do nothin' wrong. Right there's the nub of it. *He can't do nothin' wrong.*"

He stamped off through the batwings still carrying the kid's hat.

5

RHODE Island Red, after his painful and humiliating eviction from the saloon, got up out of the dirt and hunted blasphemously around until he found the pistol Brett had heaved through the window.

His right knee was skinned, the left sleeve of his checked coat was out at the elbow, and he was still spitting mud in a frustrated fury. But he was not enough out of his head to attempt to fire off that gun without cleaning it.

Fasken would keep. There were other things more urgent. He didn't want any more of these local yokels seeing him. That business just now would be stretched and spread far enough without further embellishments.

Dragging himself up onto the horse he thought of something else he'd better do. He cuffed the horse's head through the Red Wall's doors and said his piece and whirled back out.

The thought of Fasken's sister back at the ranch made him feel a little better; nevertheless he roweled the bronc a solid half mile before he eased up on him. These Faskens! By God they were really something!

Imagine that bastard showing his face around here! At least Jo wouldn't know about it—yet. Christ! Red had only come in by chance. He might have gone right on, never knowing. But he knew now!

Might have to change his plans a little; nothing he couldn't take care of though. He'd just got to speed things up, was all. Good thing, maybe. He was goddam tired bobbing around for that old biddy—Yes, ma'am! No, ma'am! Enough to make a guy puke! He'd known Injuns could do it better. Why, he'd as soon, by God, get in bed with a cow—but that was all right, too! Playing for the top of the heap a man had to expect to put up with a few things. It wasn't like the old fool was going to be around forever!

Red let that thought soak into him. He played around with the notion for a couple of miles while he cursed at his bruises and damned Brett Fasken and all his tribe. She could be got at all right, but there was a risk about the business a man didn't have to take—not a man smart as Red who had parlayed hard luck into a mighty pleasing prospect. Besides, he didn't know yet if she had changed her will or not.

She'd been going too, all right, but his experience with women —and now here was Fasken back horning in where nobody by God wanted him. Maybe Red had better get her into double harness.

He studied that over for the next several horse lengths without coming to any definite conclusion. He saw a number of drawbacks, but he would do it if he had to. He had plenty of time to make up his mind; by the shortest way it was a four-hour ride to Hobbled O. But when he pulled up to the door he'd damn well better know most of the answers because there was still Bill Tice to reckon with. Be going on for ten but she'd be up—you could bet on that!

He didn't want her seeing him all tore up. She had a horror of blood. He remembered them two mozos he had gunned, and that drifter he'd pistol-whipped—she'd like to never let up on that. Might be a good notion to let her see how Brett had—

The thought was tempting but he put it away from him. Smarter to keep Fasken clean out of this. She might not have much use for her brother but blood was thicker than water, and when it came to a showdown there was one thing his experience had taught him—it was to never, by Jesus, tie faith up in a woman!

He couldn't keep Fasken out of this indefinitely—not without chancing considerable more than Red wanted to think about.

It all came back to that damned old biddy. No john who was known to have cut down her brother was going to be standing in line for that goddam ranch!

So maybe he had ought to blow the whistle on Brett, let her have a good look at what her brother had done to him, piling it on every way he could, showing her what loyalty had made Red take on her behalf. Looked a pretty good bet, spread on thick or played down. Might even make him look good to Tice.

He sure didn't want Brett sucking around, getting back in her good graces. Handled right this might be the means of getting that will changed. Red had a lot of influence with her—not as much as he'd have liked but nobody realized that up till now. Nobody knew he hadn't been able to displace Bill Tice as Hobbled O's big auger or make the bastard quit. But Tice wasn't pulling no wool over *his* eyes! The cold-jawed segundo was after the same thing Red was and—except for Red—might have damned well got it!

It wasn't Tice who was threatening Red's prospects; Tice could be taken care of. His allegiance to the outfit was all that was keeping Bill Tice above ground. A pile of things could happen to a man working with cattle and one of these days . . . It was that goddam Brett!

Well, Brett could be taken care of too. Might be some sticky ground to get over but a man with what it took in his thinkbox was bound to come up with two or three answers, and Jo couldn't hold a guy off forever. An accident could happen to her as well as Tice, and a damned sight weller if a feller was minded to make it. She was hooked and going to be feeling the need of it and once an old biddy starts playing with fire it's pretty generally safe figuring she's going to get burnt. When she did she was going to have to do something about it, and sure as Red got her up in front of the gospel no matter how bitter Fasken might grind his teeth there wasn't one goddam thing he could do.

He sure as hell couldn't pot his own sister's husband and expect to come in for any part of Hobbled O!

6

BRETT stared after the departing marshal. Never convince these fools Jo hadn't sent for him. Shock was wearing out of them now and you could tell by the way they were looking at him they'd pegged this humbling of Red as a put-up job.

Jo wouldn't take no lip off him either. She'd reckon the only thing could have fetched him back was the prospect of cutting into her pie—and Jo had to be *thought* about. If this bunch didn't take care of his hash she'd be bustin a gut to run him off.

Schrader, lips thinning, reached up his sawed-off and set it on the bar.

Brett got out of there.

There was a lot more traffic on the street, more wagons, more horses. The town was filling up and this wasn't no pay day unless the spreads around here had changed their schedule. Not caring to encounter any additional familiar faces he pushed along the rumbling walk, passing up the old Home Cooked Grub and turning tight-mouthed into the Omaha Café.

There were five or six gabbers pushing food into their faces. Brett didn't know any of them. He slouched onto a stool at the counter and gave his order. When the grub came he ate it, went back and got his horse and tied him to the barber's pole. There were two fellers waiting and one being worked on. The guy with the scissors was new to him. "Any room in the tub?"

The barber looked him over. "You'll hev to pump your own water—an' mind that handle. She ain't too stout."

Brett nodded, hung up his hat and went through the rear door. When he came back a half hour later the only customer in sight was the one that was being shaved. When the chair was empty Brett got into it. "I'll take the full course." He got to thinking of the way this town had filled up. "You have this much of a mob around every day?"

"Nope. They got a meetin' tonight."

"That so?" Brett said after a moment, "What kind of a meetin'?"

"Cattleman's. Don't recollect seein' your face before."

"Can't say as I remember flappin' eyes at you either."

Brett said it so crusty the man stepped back, staring.

"Hell," he said, taking in the wide shoulders, the smoldering look boring into him—"don't git me wrong, Jack. Just making conversation."

"You've made it," Brett said. "Get busy."

But later Brett's need for information made him ask while the man was stropping his razor, "What's the chances of getting on around here?"

"Poorly."

"Account of this drought?"

"That's part of it."

"Money's tight, eh? All cuttin' down?"

The barber said, trying his blade out, "Hobbled O and Currycomb is still eatin' regular. But some of them boys is pinchin' the bottom of the barrel." He scraped off the lather around Brett's ear.

"What about them first two?"

"Friend, you better ask them about that."

When the man wiped his razor and tossed the wet towel into a bucket Brett said, getting up, "I'm a pretty good bronc stomper. You might pass the word around."

The man, looking away from him, nodded. Brett paid him and went over and put on his hat. "If it's the best I can get I'll break them on shares."

The barber, staring out of the window, said, "Might try Scab 8."

Brett said "Thanks," and went out.

He was thoughtful, climbing into the saddle, and he sat there a while still pushing it around. The face and shape of that girl were sharp in his head. Able had suggested he try Scab 8 too, but the storekeeper probably hoped Trone would put a bullet through him.

Someway Brett didn't feel so depressed. The prospect of renewing his brief acquaintance with Lola had nothing to do with it. There was the germ of a fourteen-carat idea floating around through his thoughts and if he could just get his choppers sunk deep enough into it. . . .

Night was falling fast as Brett kneed his flaxen-haired roan across the road and pushed him into the westbound traffic. He edged him up behind a lumbering freighter, still thoughtful but keeping his eyes skinned. If there was any real truth in this notion of Jo trying to drop a long loop about those folks at Scab 8 he could damn well show this bunch around here he'd no intention of dancing to whatever tune she piped. He guessed McInery could tell him. Come as near to the truth as Brett was anxious to get.

Where buildings came vaguely out of this crosshatch of light and fluttering shadow Brett cut the roan hard right onto a runway. He didn't expect to help swallow any fatted calf but it did kind of seem like he might discover which way the wind blew. He didn't figure to look too closely into this because Jo, if it suited her, could get up her back over nothing at all and he had trouble enough now.

As he came into the reach of the barn entrance lantern the gaunt stoop-shouldered shape of the Scot came out of the blackness and stood with crossed arms, dour and immutable. "No room for you here, Fasken."

"Same old Mac," Brett said with a chuckle. "Still remembering that wall—"

"There's no room for ye here!"

The hard burr of his tone was expected but Brett hadn't looked for him to turn down a dollar. "Hell," he said, "this bronc ain't et yet."

"Aye. Ye never was one to worry aboot dumb animals wi' the charnst o' a cloutin' takin' up yer whole outlook."

Brett's eyes narrowed. "So you've heard about Red. Well, it's no skin off your nose—"

"Be skin off in plenty afore ye git done wi' this."

"You don't mind givin' the horse a drink do you?"

McInery motioned them over to a trough. "Don't gi' off him."

"Put some oats in a nosebag too, while you're at it."

The Scot went grumbling off into the dark. He could talk a pretty fair brand of English when his dander wasn't up. Brett let the roan drink, reckoning the horse was cool enough now; it was the coolness of McInery he couldn't quite fathom. The old man hadn't ever had much use for him, but this went beyond that—even beyond Red, by the looks of it.

McInery came back and handed up the morral. "Dollar twenty. Take it wi' ye."

Brett passed him the silver. The roan, swinging his head around, nickered for the oats. Brett, still considering McInery, kept the bag out of his reach. "What's chewin' you, Mac?"

"If a man needed reason you're reason enough," a harsh voice exclaimed behind Brett through a metallic chinging of spurs. "You just can't keep out of trouble, can you!"

Brett, twisting around, found Tice's stare blackly gouging him. There had always been this quality to the man, a quietness that—to Brett, at least—bordered on insolence, a kind of overbearing assurance that went beyond the rights of a ramrod as though whatever Bill Tice chose to say or think transcended dispute and was—for other men—law.

It had always rubbed Brett the wrong way, whipping up his own intolerance. Now it made him say with calculated malice, "Oh—that you, Tice?" and turn his back indifferently to look again at McInery. "Thought maybe you might know of someone needin' a good hand with their horse stock."

Through McInery's silence Brett heard the hard tramp of the Hobbled O segundo's boots coming at him. Not until the man had practically reached his stirrup did Brett give any sign that he knew of Tice's fury. Turning then, he said, "What's chewin' you?"

"There's no jobs here and if there was you wouldn't get 'em —you understand that? Jo don't want you around. I don't want you around, either. Now if you've got any sense—"

"I never did have," Brett grinned. "Ask Mac."

He got out his Durham. Tice, lunging forward, batted it out of his hand. Brett shook a boot loose. Tice jumped back and whipped out his gun. His eyes dared Brett to start something.

Brett softly laughed. "Well," he said to the liveryman, picking up his reins, "expect I better be siftin' along."

"You better be sifting right out of this country," Tice told him, ugly, "if you want to keep healthy."

Brett said to McInery, "Might be Trone could use a extry hand. Hear he's got some stuff needs gentlin'."

The Scott, blank of face, kept his jaws hard shut, but the eyes of Josephine's segundo blazed with uncontrollable hatred. He was a man who could not endure resistance. His heavily mustached face suddenly darkened with fury. "Do that," he said, "and you're dead," and stamped away from them.

7

SOME hundred rods from the livery Brett got out of the saddle in a vacant lot across from the Coffin Bar and, removing his gear, curried the horse with that unflagging zeal a man mostly shows when in a spirit of penance he attempts belatedly to make up for something. Then be gave the horse the oats and sucked his pipe while he waited.

The night was still hot. No breeze came out of the shadows to relieve the oppressive closeness of the air. It carried the smell of scorched earth, reminding Brett of the drought and of his sister's alleged plans; and thinking of these things he caught the drift of sounds coming past the blaze of the Rochester lamps that brightened every opening of the honkytonk yonder: guitar sounds and fiddle squeals with an occasional isolated voice cutting through them and, once, a woman's high laugh, fetching Lola's face and blue velvet eyes up out of the dissatisfied grind of his thoughts.

The place was too still. There was no jostle of movement beyond the bright oblongs of undraped windows, no crowd at the bar. Brett took a long look around and with a grunt of impatience bent and picked up the blanket, shaking it irascibly before dropping it and smoothing it into place behind the horse's withers. He saddled up, took off the bag, rebitted the roan, and got aboard. "Grass won't grow," he told the horse, "if you stand on it," and, suddenly snorting, he put the animal into the near-empty street.

He didn't have to look long before he found what he was hunting. Most of the rigs and tied horses were congregated about the schoolhouse. He walked the roan in that direction. This wasn't what he wanted but it was plain he wouldn't be let alone around here and he was damned if he would run. This thing he had made up his mind to probably wasn't the best choice but he had to get some of this bunch off his neck.

There was a pretty fair crowd, mostly punchers and towns-men, in the Red Wall. But here too, as at the Coffin Bar, there seemed considerably less noise than was natural. There were still a few wagons at the Mercantile, but what customers he could see were all women. His mouth drew in a bit more at the corners and he wondered if perhaps he hadn't better strap on his gun. But this was not the time or the place for guns. The last thing Brett wanted was to have to kill anyone.

He had thought coming back here was going to make a free man of him. He wondered now if anyone ever was truly free. Then he put these thoughts away from him, his attention swing-ing out of habit to the heavier patches of shadow, the door holes and alleys, the indeterminate sounds coming out of the night.

He passed through trees, climbed a slight grade, and found the schoolhouse before him. Leaving the roan on dropped reins among a huddle of other horses he pushed through the clutter of rigs, seeing the women and kids stiffly sitting in some of them. Small owner families, he guessed. Big augers didn't fetch their womenfolks to business.

A group of squatting men, silent at his approach, thickened the shadows below the railed porch. He could feel their curious stares as he moved through them and stonily mounted the steps. The single red eye of a hand-rolled burned in front of the glass-less door which stood closed, like the windows, although it was hot enough to melt bear grease.

The burning eye went pinwheeling over the rail, marking its discarder either as a greenhorn or a damned careless man. Brett, caught in the butter-yellow flood from the windows, couldn't see much more than the general shape of him against that black door.

The man said bluntly, "You can turn around now and climb back down with the—"

"Maybe," Brett smiled, "I've got business in there."

"It can wait till they're through then. This hassayampa's private. Turn around."

Brett casually but firmly thrust the man to one side, stepping through the door before the fellow could take up enough slack to stop him.

Tice had been talking; he broke off in midflow, and stared angrily at Brett. "You've got the wrong place. This is an Association meetin'. For cattlemen," he said pointedly.

"I thought my sister owned Hobbled O."

"She does," Tice snapped, not seeing that Brett had put the words in his mouth. "I'm speakin' for her. You've got no stake here, Fasken."

There were perhaps ten men in the smoky room. Flagler, the Currycomb owner, was sardonically watching from his perch on a desk some ten paces from Tice. The rest of the bunch, a raggedy-pants outfit, were huddled like sheep over against one of the windows.

It was these small owners Brett was trying to reach. He had to disassociate himself from Hobbled O. He had to do it in such a way that some of these men would see that the word got around. He said now to Tice, "Not a stake maybe but I've certainly got a voice—"

"Talkin' for who?"

"Trone," Brett said. "I'm representin' Scab 8."

Every man in the room went still but Tice. The Hobbled O segundo shook his head like a bee-stung bear. Flagler grinned, watching Tice. Ollie Schultz, whom Brett had imagined to have gone home after his hysterics at the Red Wall, showed an open disbelief that bordered on the ludicrous. Several of the men nearest him attempted to edge inconspicuously back.

"Trone has no voice," Tice growled with blunt finality.

"Owns cattle, don't he?"

"That's a matter of opinion."

"Whose opinion!" Brett bit back at him. And, when Tice did not answer, Brett raked the rest of them. "What kind of a pass has this country come to when a feller packin' a grudge can brand his neighbor a thief an' then deny the poor bastard even a chance to be heard?"

"Trone hasn't tried to be heard!" Tice shouted furiously "He's been warned!" He shook his fists, glaring around, hammering at that flutter of small owners. "We're here to rule Scab 8 off the range. Now let's get it done! All in favor—"

"Your word—even speakin' for Josephine," Brett said, "don't carry that much weight. As Trone's rep I've got a right—"

"You're here on sufferance," yelled Tice, swelling up, "you got no rights at all!" Fists clenched he plowed toward Brett, his eyes like a crazy man's.

"Just a minute." That was Flagler.

Tice pulled up. He threw a look over his shoulder, demanding incredulously, "You sidin' that trash?"

"Currycomb's not taking sides—yet." Flagler's sardonic glance swept over all of them. A kind of grudging quiet came over the room. Tice scowled, and the bunch by the window resettled into a thin hold on hope.

Flagler said, "Nobody's doubting there's stuff being stolen. I been missing a few here and there myself. That don't have to mean Trone's been getting them." He pushed out a silencing hand at Tice. "Nobody's questioning your sincerity, Bill, but that's no proof you've got the straight of it. If you'd caught him red-handed that would be somethin' else. I'm as down on rustlers as anybody could be, but—" He stopped and, shrugging, said instead, "There's like to be trouble we go pushing Vic into this."

"Trouble!" Tice snorted. "We got trouble now!" His eyes skewered Brett. "This galoot's never been anythin' *but* trouble! If he's teamed up with Trone—"

"Is that what's back of your sweat to get rid of Vic?"

Tice swung his head like a badgered bull. "No one but a plumb fool would ever doubt who's puttin' wings t' these critters! Drunk half the time—look where his place is at! I don't need no more than to look at his brand to know by God where my cows're goin'!" He flung a savage glance at the bunch by the window. "I'm callin' for a show of hands. Right now! Them that's for puttin' Trone out shove your fists up."

One or two seemed reluctant but all put their hands up.

"That settles it." Tice glared at Flagler. He looked minded to say more but Brett took the play away.

"All right. You've put him out. He still owns stock—"

Tice shouted, "All Trone owns is what acres he's filed on! He'll sell an' sell fast or git planted right there. You can't run an outlawed brand in this country! Anythin' packin' his mark is fair meat for the first iron that gits to it!"

"This Jo's idea or yours?" Brett said.

Tice's face mottled with insufferable fury. He sprang at Fasken, grabbing out his pistol, but Brett, suddenly straightening inside the man's swing, brought the slicing edge of his left hand hard against Tice's neck. As the burly range boss staggered, Brett's outstabbing right, clamping onto that thick wrist, yanked it brutally up behind Tice's·shoulder blade. Tice bellowed, his eyes popping, and the gun fell out of his fist.

"Whose idea was it?" Brett demanded.

Tice wasn't cowed. Unaccustomed to resistance, the agony he'd experienced had shook a little sense into him. "Mine," he growled shortly, and picked up his hat. Then—he couldn't have abided himself otherwise—he said with the hate snarling out of his words: "He'll sell or git planted! You go out there you'll git planted with him!"

Brett grinned at him bleakly, and his look included Flagler. "You better think some more about that before you try it."

8

WHEN Tice got back to the ranch a light was still brightening the drawn shades of the office windows. The Hobbled O segundo tossed his reins at one of his men and went striding in the direction of a showdown. Josephine wasn't going to be pleased with what he had to say. She wasn't going to like being bothered if that whelp of a kid was in there, but when it came to matters concerning the welfare of Hobbled O the segundo's word still carried considerable weight. How she would take this would probably hinge on whether or not Red was with her and what, if anything, he'd already told her.

Tice stepped onto the gallery and went along to the door, batting a hand impatiently against it. "Come in," Josephine's voice called, and that rankled in him too, the unimaginative, wholly confident sound of it, as though welcoming unheralded knockers into the house at this time of the night were the most natural thing in the world.

He flung the door open, slamming it back of him.

She looked at him coolly. She was alone, fully dressed, with her boots on, and she appeared to have been reading. She had a book closed around one finger and was garbed like a man in brush-clawed range clothes, the top three buttons of her shirt carelessly open. Her cut-short hair that had once been red and now resembled rained-on wood ash affronted more than usual his conception of the fit and proper. It seemed to him that sometimes Jo Fasken went out of her way to appear obnoxious.

She was full-breasted, deep-breasted, with unfettered hips and

37

a waist whose girth, even now, was substantially less than what Tice's belt had to go around. She had the kind of face a good sculptor might have brought out of rock with a dull chisel. Its lines, faintly blurred, conveyed an air of past grandeur peculiarly patrician and inescapably formidable. There was still something handsome about this frowsy old woman. It wasn't that she was so *old*—not rightly. More the way that unshaded shine from the lamp caught hold of and harshened the network of wrinkles that some nights a man was hard put to find. If she'd taken any kind of care of herself. . . .

She never bothered to greet a man. She invariably spoke as though continuing a subject already hashed over, and now said in a kind of sour amusement, "Can't you sleep, either?"

Tice gestured sharply. She knew he'd just gotten in. Anyone else with as much at stake would have been hounding him with questions about that meeting. Jo Fasken seldom could be accused of the obvoius—except, Tice thought, in the case of that kid. Red was making a fool of her.

Tice was angry, and the way her glance kept sliding around to the side of his neck didn't help matters. He said, "They've kicked Trone out."

"Of course," she smiled. "What else could they do? I suppose Flagler put in his two bits' worth? He's bound not to like—"

"You better listen to me. Trone's got him some help. Brett's back."

He waited to see how she'd take it, and he was a little put out she didn't jump from her chair or catch a hand to her throat— any other woman would have. But when had Jo Fasken ever been like other women?

Tice could remember when she'd been a heap more like them; before that goddam Brett. . . . Tice pushed the thought away from him. Her face hadn't revealed the least sign of surprise. The kid, Tice reckoned, must have already told her; then he wasn't so sure. And increased flatness showed in her eyes.

Tice said, "He was at the meetin'. Claimed to be reppin' for Trone."

If she was jarred she didn't show it. "Brett always was a damned fool," she said. "It's that girl, of course. I'll have a talk with him."

Tice said, "You better hear the rest of it." He gave her a close-up of the meeting, including the promise he himself had made of what Brett could look for if Hobbled O came up with him.

She said composedly, "Well, he's been warned. What did Stoker have to say? Busy shining his badge was he?"

"He wasn't at the school—oh! You mean about Brett? I don't guess he's puttin' any flags out."

She said after a moment, "We can do some thinking about it. We don't want Flagler getting into this, Bill."

"He ain't blind," Tice growled. "He's bound to see that once we've taken over . . ."

"That's not proof. We've got to keep him rooted while we pick up these spreads."

"We can handle him."

"We can't handle him with Brett stirring up those greasy-sackers—not that I think Brett will, but he may try."

"I'd say he was tryin' pretty hard right now!"

Josephine smiled in her dry parch-lipped way and it got into him that behind her mask she was furious. She let a little of this get into her tone, saying abruptly, "I wish you'd kept your damned mouth shout. Tell me everything you've heard about what went on before that meeting. How long was Brett around? Who talked to him? What was the sense of it?"

The segundo went over it. "Well," she said a little more companionably, "I guess we've found out enough to show what quarter the wind's in. Long as the records show Hobbled O belongs half to Brett there's not like to be many who will trust him farther than they'd be able to heave him. We just don't want to have our hands too full. Pin the rustling on Trone and Flagler'll stay out of this."

He looked at her carefully. "You really believe that?"

"Long enough," she said, twisting her mouth at him. "We've still got that town by the seat of the pants. They may not like us but they'll stay in line; the banker, the butcher, the baker—"

"What butcher?"

"Don't be so impossibly literal." She yawned. "Red come in with you?"

Red was one thing he hadn't wanted to talk about, being a subject he could hardly trust himself with. "You mean he ain't back yet?"

Almost imperceptibly she stiffened. He was on thin ice and he could sense the sway of it. All the arguments he'd ever had with her had stemmed directly out of that kid. "Did Red have trouble with Brett?"

Tice edged a look at her. "He got a little mouthy."

He could see her eyes flattening, the pinched sharpness of her nostrils. She said at last, "What happened?"

"Brett throwed him out of Schrader's." He told her about it, making a point of the fact that he himself had not been there.

She put down her book. She got up out of the chair and moved about the narrow room, her face expressionless as one of Schrader's poker checks.

"I wouldn't worry about it none," he said. "If he was able to git up he's able to git home."

She swiveled bleak eyes and their stare went right through him. "Don't talk like a fool!"

There were some aspects of her connection with that kid he didn't want to understand, but he savvied enough to guess pretty accurately what kind of pictures she was calling up now. What the kid had done took her back to the night Brett had told her Clint Wilder was dead. She was probably seeing him standing over Red with what was left of that goddam wrecked chair in his hands. She hadn't got around yet to remembering the men Red had killed, to seeing the kid's sneering face wreathed in gun smoke.

Josephine said thickly, "He's got to get out of here!"

Tice didn't know which one of them she meant but he said, "Yeah," enormously encouraged at the idea of being rid of either. Both would have been better.

9

BRETT remembered the Aravaipa as a tributary of the San Pedro River, having confluence with it some eight to ten miles below Winkelman and with its source someplace in the neighborhood of Bonita, a long day's ride from Packer's Crossing. A mighty long day's ride, he thought while the roan plodded north through a night filled with stars. Brett had no idea whereabouts in that rugged country Trone's Scab 8 holdings were located and, since he hadn't considered it prudent to ask, he was faced with the prospect of following the creek's convolutions through a good many miles of mountains without he wanted to ask around at Bonita or chance hitting one of the settlements farther west or north.

He could stick with the river to Cascabel, but if no one knew there the next chance was Redington and it might be as much as ten miles out of the way. If he stayed clear of these gossip points and kept straight on north he might save considerable time and, by bearing east just a little, come into Sunset, some twelve miles west by a couple of whoops south of Bonita. He decided this was probably the most sensible course and figured he'd likely arrive just about getting-up time.

He wasn't at all sure he was doing the right thing hunting Trone, but the look of Trone's sister was still in his mind and it was dollars to doughnuts no one else would put him on. Trone might not, either. Whether or not he was stealing cattle he'd have precious little reason to put any trust in a Fasken. Both the barber and Able had suggested Trone might hire him, and maybe the man would if he was desperate enough. But Brett had a hunch they'd been steering him at Trone to get him out from under foot.

Trone's place was about as far as he could go and still remain in the country which had watched Brett Fasken grow up. Packer's Crossing was the biggest and southernmost town in the country, Bonita, in the shadow of Fort Grant, being the easternmost and next largest town. There weren't any other places big enough to be called towns. A rough, wild country, thinly settled and feudal. Cow country. Gun country. He would have to watch out for that kid, by the looks of him.

RHODE Island Red, after starting for Hobbled O, had changed his mind and cut directly north. His recent humiliation at Brett's hands was still coloring his thoughts but a scheme had finally come to him through which, if he played his cards right, he might recoup his damaged standing and have a good chance even of brightening his prospects—and all without personally lifting a hand against Brett. That jasper was going to rue the day. . . .

Red hugged this thought all through the night. The scheme he'd stumbled onto was likely to pay off a good many debts and do it with no blame to him; but first he wanted a talk with Lola Trone. She'd cold-shouldered him right from the first and yet. . . . Merely thinking about her was enough to start the fire in him. If she gave him the grand duchess treatment again he would make Trone sweat.

At two in the morning he skirted Sunset, cutting up through the mountains just this side of it, moving slowly now and with all the caution he was able to manage. He didn't want to encounter anyone who might later recall and maybe mention having seen him. No telling what might come of this trip, and if things worked out. . . . It brought the sweat out on him just thinking about her.

He camped as soon as he got out of the mountains, not to rest his hard-breathing horse but to hold to the schedule he'd laid out for himself. He wanted Trone to be gone when he got there and the middle of the morning was the most likely time. Two things Red didn't consider; he didn't know the girl had been in Packer's Crossing or that Brett, at the schoolhouse, had said he was working for Trone. Either one of these facts, had he known, would have changed his plans considerably.

He didn't have food so he didn't need a fire. He left his horse on trailing reins and curled up for two hours, hat over face, in a covert of brush. It was full light when he awakened. He found the horse, still saddled, close by, what quantity and caliber of grass were here available having constituted no threat to the discipline of dropped reins. He tested the girth and got aboard. By this time the sun was up.

Going to be another scorcher. The Graham Mountains were ahead and to the right of him. A haze like drifted wood smoke ranged halfway up the slopes of Merrill Peak and the Winchesters, off to the south, already looked blue as turquoise. If this drought didn't break pretty soon there wouldn't nobody have any grass left to speak of.

He put these things out of mind, returning his quickening thoughts to Lola Trone. She had rebuffed every advance he'd made in her direction but his experiences with women assured him he had made no mistake about her and this conjured visions which mightily excited him. His conquest of Jo had not lived up to expectations, hadn't been worth the tedious care that had gone into it or the restraint that had kept him stalking weeks longer than results had warranted. He sneered at the knowledge gained of her even though half his scheme was predicated on it. This Trone girl was younger; the fires weren't banked, only hidden.

He hoped her drunken brother was gone because he'd rather not—all things considered—have to put a bullet through him. It wasn't as though anyone would give a damn. Trone, sober, was too much of a loner ever to have made any friends in this country. Red didn't see what they had to be so all-fired proud about! Even in Bonita, which got most of their trade, they weren't noticeably better than on nodding terms with anyone.

He licked his lips and recalled how he had put in Jo's mind the conviction Vic Trone was the one who'd been getting away with their cattle. Hadn't been too hard with the rest of them small johns scraping and bowing—even, by Christ, to the goddam punchers she had on her payroll! Enough to make a man puke; but Trone hadn't bowed. He hadn't cared about anything.

So what was there to worry about? This whole thing was set up for him. With Tice backing Jo's notions about Trone and the whole damned outfit spreading it for him nobody was going to get into no sweat if Trone was found plugged and the girl. . . . Some might feel a little uneasy about her but without any witnesses— Hell! a few casual words dropped in the right place would take care of that, and maybe Brett along with it.

Brett was a natural—any feller with Brett's rep, newly come back and all. Trone by now had been thrown out of the Association, his brand outlawed. Fasken doings, and Brett was a Fasken. Roughest one of the pack, according to tell. So what was more natural than him, still fuming, going out to their place and settling up personal for the steers they stole? The whole country would believe it. If there was any hereafter tacked onto this business Brett would damn well inherit it—along with his share of the rest of Hobbled O!

Red grinned maliciously. Things could always be worked out if a man would put a little thought to them. He felt a whole lot better. It might not even have to go that far—the part about Lola. It lay with her—he wasn't unreasonable. Could be a good thing for her. He had standing in this country, the run of Hobbled O.

It wasn't like he was some saddle bum, some john without a pot. When Rhode Island Red talked men around here were in the habit of listening, and they had by God better be! He could do things for her, maybe dress her in silk before he got done with this.

He wiped the sweat off his face and forgot about food. Forgot to curse the scorched heat that curled around him like cigar smoke. He put a heel against his horse and by the time Trone's buildings pushed into view had sold himself into a fine lather of impatience.

There was smoke coming out of the shack's tin chimney and he reckoned she was cooking. He cocked a glance at the sun. A good hour yet till noon and no sign of Trone. Horses in the saddle trap but none caught up or waiting. Without the son of a bitch was drunk inside he must be gone just like Red had reckoned he would be.

He rode into the yard feeling seven feet tall and got down in front of the rickety porch. More out of habit than for any better reason his hand touched the gun that was under his armpit; there wasn't anything to worry him. Trone had no help and Red saw no sign of neighbors. His heart was pounding as he took the first step. A rattling of pans came through the open door.

She hadn't heard him. He put a hand against a post and moved up onto the rotten porch.

10

IT was crowding six when Brett drew rein before the cross-trails store that was the hub of Sunset and briefly stared at the conglomeration of clackety shacks tiredly clinging like scabrous growth to the roundabout slopes. Even at this altitude the vagrant breeze had no real life to it, and the bright glare of sun pushing its face above the purple rim of the Pinalenos extended no hope the day held anything better.

A pouchy man in an unbuttoned hickory shirt and torn jeans came out of the door with a bucket in his fist, caught sight of Brett and stopped, undecided, to paw a hand through hair which stood up every whichway. "Lookin' fer somebody?"

"I'd settle for a meal," Brett said, "if one was handy."

The fellow scratched his hairy chest and upended the bucket over a knife-scarred rail, splattering the adjacent ground with his slops without once taking his eyes off Brett. His stare was questioning.

"Bronc stomper," Brett told him. "Headin' for the Aravaipa to see if I can turn up some work."

"Cash is some scarcer'n hens' teeth."

"I ain't proud," Brett smiled. "I'll take whatever." When the fellow still stood there indecisively Brett said, still on his horse, "I ain't lookin' for no hand-outs."

"Well—git down," the man said without any great warmth. "Hay's around back an' water's in the tank. I'll see what I kin throw together. Likely won't be much but it'll settle your gut a mite, mebbe."

47

Brett swing down. "Do I come in when I'm ready?"

"I ain't takin' it out there."

There was a corral behind the place and, after pulling his gear and watching the animal roll, Brett left the roan inside the poles and fetched a couple of armfuls of hay from the nearer of three weathered stacks. Then he cuffed himself off, washed up at the tank, ran wet fingers through his hair and tramped back.

Smell of woodsmoke blended pleasantly with coffee smell and cooking hog above the variety of odors commonly found in a country store. Brett got out his pipe on the porch and went in. He found the sacked tobacco and picked up a couple and the man came out of a door with his breakfast and put it down on the bar that flanked the far side of the room. "Four bits," he said with his eyes on the tobacco.

Brett paid him and tried the coffee. It was strong enough to walk and hot enough to defeather an eagle but it wasn't like anything he'd tasted before. "Jamoka," the hairy one said with a scowl. "Ain't it good enough fer you?"

"Slips down mighty easy," Brett nodded, and dug in. Besides the coffee and side meat there were refried potatoes with considerable black in them and a thick slab of mush. And two biscuits that had obviously been around longer than Brett had.

When he'd cleaned out the plate Brett loaded his pipe. The man was still watching him, perched on a counter with his shirt still unbuttoned and his pale little eyes never missing a wink.

Brett said tentatively, "Know a feller named Trone?"

"Be another six bits for the hay," the man said.

"Heard he might have some broncs could stand a little work on 'em. If you could give me some idea where he lived," Brett explained, "I figured I might look him up." He laid three quarters on the bar.

The man considered him, turning it over. "Straight north," he said finally. "Eighteen mile."

"Obliged," Brett said, putting a match to his pipe. He felt the storekeeper's eyes, as he left, still following him. He gave the roan a drink and saddled up and set off.

He did a heap of thinking without improving his mood. By all the signs and signal smokes no one but a simon-pure idiot would push this thing one whisker further.

Those who knew him didn't want him around and the rest of these people distrusted strangers on general principles. He wouldn't be at all surprised if that eighteen miles straight north took him nowhere near the place he was aiming for. He had thought, by his stand at that association meeting, to clear the air a little; but all he'd done had been to stir up more trouble. He could still see Flagler's knowing grin, the bitter stare of Ollie Schultz. Not one of them had shown him the faintest sign of trust, and that business of him and Bill Tice locking horns hadn't helped him a particle.

Couldn't much blame them for eying him slanchways. Nor for the fears that kept gnawing them—*any* of them. The hazards of raising cattle were obnoxious enough under the best of conditions. The big cowman didn't live who could draw comfort or pleasure from the prospect of neighboring with any bunch of starving squatters. Nor could such a one entertain anything more than open suspicion for another big owner feeding off the same graze and coolly bound in the same direction. In the very nature of the things he was up against a man had either to push or see himself frozen out.

Small owners had to make it any way they could. Some of them, like enough, had come into this country honest, but a man with a family to provide for was bound to find honesty a pretty dubious virtue without enough on the table to keep body and soul together. Mostly men hankered to do the right thing but sometimes that thing could get pretty well hidden. They were scared and without any kind of security and it was going to get worse. Made desperate enough some were bound to get killed. Every man caught in this bind savvied that much.

Right now they were eating out of Hobbled O's hand but this move against Trone could go either way. Designed to discourage, it could also unite them, pointing up what could happen if they didn't stick together. Right now they were scared, decrying any connection with a man who'd incurred Jo's wrath.

Flagler wasn't scared. Been no sign the man was even much worried. Brett was sure, however, the Currycomb boss correctly assessed what its bigger neighbor was up to. He'd have guessed; no man having eyes sharp as Flagler would miss understanding of what could happen to Currycomb once Tice was free to give it undivided attention. Hobbled O wasn't going to be at heart really happy sharing anything with anyone.

Brett shook his head. Bound to be blood spilled and no amount of stubbornness on his part could stop it—didn't even much seem like it would cut down the odds any. Pretty generally he could manage to hit what he aimed at but nobody was going to be out much sleep worrying about what Brett Fasken could do with a gun.

The marshal had warned him. Ollie Schultz, half crazy with fear, had warned him; that feisty kid. Tice, too, he remembered gloomily. He did a strange thing then. He leanly smiled. Better for this bunch if they had shot him down at once.

Suddenly impatient he lifted the roan into faster movement. A man couldn't see very far ahead of him sometimes. He had to take whatever came and do the best he could with it. A lot was going to depend on Trone, on what Trone thought of him and what Trone decided. Lola's brother was the key to this. Would he fight or bolt?

LOLA Trone with a long-handled pot in one hand stuck her head out the door just as Rhode Island Red came up onto the porch. Startled surprise froze her there. Then her mouth pulled down and there was contempt in her look. "What's the matter with you—lost?"

It threw Red a little off balance and while he was trying to find a suitable reply she said, pointing: "Hobbled O's off there— off behind that lemon-colored hill. Climb back on your horse and start putting down tracks."

Red sneered, then grinned boldly. She wasn't fooling him any. His eyes traveled over her body. He suddenly laughed at the gone- still look of her, at the blood pounding into her face, at her quick fury.

She drew back as he started toward her, the show of fright in her eyes bringing up the sap in him, shearing off the last thin hampering of caution. He'd waited a long while for a chance like this. Chuckling deep in his throat he sprang after her.

Her eyes were like holes burned through a board with hot iron. In a continuous motion she let go of the pot, ducked under his outstreched hand and brought up a rifle that was inside the room. Red got hold of the barrel, swearing, twisting it away from him, savagely wrenching it out of her hands. He flung it into the yard and, thoroughly aroused, grabbed as she tried, too late, to spin away from him.

He caught a fistful of yellow hair and yanked her around and slammed her into the wall. She struck back at him, frantic. He cuffed her hard across the face. She reeled into the table and the table went over and he caught her before she could regain her balance. She tried to get at his eyes. He grabbed the front of her dress and ripped it almost to her navel.

Across the room someone said, "You son of a bitch!" and Red, shocked cold sober, saw Trone, puffy-faced, coming out of a bedroom.

Trone, by the looks, had been hitting a bottle. As though in confirmation one of his empty hands came uncertainly up to clutch at the jamb, steadying him there while his bloodshot eyes,

increasingly ugly, fastened on Red as if to tear him limb from limb.
"You son of a bitch!" he said again and started, bear clumsy, across
the room.

Red turned loose and thrust a hand inside his coat. "No!"
Lola cried. Red's hand jerked back into sight, flame roaring out of
it. Trone, banging into a table leg, was flung half around by the
bullet's impact and collapsed like an emptied sack.

The girl was onto Red then, a hellcat of fury, scratching, claw-
ing, beating her fists into him, driving him backward. He tried to
club her with the gun and she got hold of it, dragging his arm
down, anchoring her weight to it, bringing him over, sinking her
teeth in him. He used his left fist on her, uncaringly, frantic.

No wonder, in all of this noise and confusion, neither of
them saw the blurred shape cross the porch or stand black in the
doorhole. Not even when, lunging inside, he stood over them was
this newcomer noticed. They were too intent, too desperately em-
broiled in their struggle for the gun. Not until his hand clubbed
down on the back of Red's neck were they aware of him, and then
only indirectly. Red's knees began to fold. His fingers let go of the
pistol. Its sudden release, the almost instant change in stress and
tension, staggered the girl's precarious balance and Red's weight,
coming down across her back, capsized her. She fell sprawling, Red
on top of her. Then his smothering weight was jerked away and,
twisting over, she saw Brett Fasken half dragging half carrying the
man through the door.

She clawed up onto her feet and, trying to cover herself,
stumbled over to Trone. That was where Fasken found her when
he came back into the house.

11

SHOCK still blurred the lumpy angles of her face and her eyes, too big, were nearly unfocused. Yet despite these things she had command of herself. With the torn dress squeezed high up against her breasts she said as though nothing in the world could be quite that important, "Will you help me get him to bed?"

Brett peered at her out of a face still unsettled. "You all right?" he said, voice flat with repression.

Color came into her face and her blue eyes fled away from him. "My bro—"

"He ain't goin' to croak if that's what you're scairt of. Get a pan, some hot water—put plenty of salt in it. Get hold of some whisky. Somethin' to tie round him."

Giving her something to do pulled her out of it. Her face tightened a little and she shuddered and got up. Her eyes even now looked a little askance at him but she went off without speaking.

Brett unbuttoned and pulled Trone's bloody shirt, baring the wound. It was in the extreme right side of his chest, low down. Still bleeding it looked ugly but he thought it unlikely to have punctured anything vital, though it was entirely possible Trone might have a cracked rib. Brett followed the rib around with his hand and found where the bullet had come out.

Trone had been lucky. Running into that table leg just as Red fired had probably saved the man's life; he certainly hadn't been hit where intended. If they could keep down infection he'd be up and around in three or four days. It was that crack on the head

53

he had got when he fell which had robbed Trone of consciousness. Luck again.

Brett studied the man, frowning. Pretty good load aboard by the smell of him. Hadn't shaved for a week—hadn't combed his hair even. He sure didn't look like no relation to Lola, but it was hard, Brett reflected, to tell much about a man when he was out. And suffering from gunshot.

A sudden thunder of hoofs spun Brett onto his feet. Crossing the room, he saw the kid's pistol and grabbed it up, reaching the porch just as Red, bent low, went pounding out of the yard and off through that patch of scraggly box elder that cut off the south view from where Brett stood. Brett, swearing, shoved the gun back of his belt and turned around.

"Got away," he said as Lola came in with the whisky. She'd fixed her dress with pins, not stopping to change. He took the strips of clean sheet from her and, considering her sideways, uncorked the bottle and held it out. "Better try some of this—"

"I'm all right."

He poked the bottle at her. "Go on, take a drag." He watched her eyes. "I'm not doin' this for me." He had a nearer knowledge of her now and thought less vaguely to understand what had fetched him here. *Was this also the reason he had gone to that meeting? Had stood up for her brother?*

Halfway affronted, more than a little astonished, he tried to find what about her had so deeply buried its barbs in him. A woman, sure, but any one of the dozen Brett had known had had looks and legs, all the commoner bait. Took more than these to bind a man. It had to be in her head—or in his.

He would have said there was nothing unusual about her but there was, he thought scowling, a peculiar undeterminedness, a kind of troubled reaching more felt than seen, a sort of searching all tangled with fears and compulsions that called up a nervous shaking inside him. Pretty weird but it was there, inexplicably exciting, and he knew beyond any doubting it had touched him the first time he'd seen her.

It was time, by God, he got out of here, time to put such thoughts completely away from him. She was just a girl with a scrambled set of values. "Go on," he said, "drink some. It'll buck you up."

She took the bottle reluctantly, considering him warily before she tilted it. Coughing she brought it hastily away, purpling, half strangled, but she looked better when she got back her breath. Brett poured some into the hole in Trone's side and, pulling him over, repeated the process.

He set the bottle aside as the unconscious man groaned. "Get the water," Brett said.

She went over to the stove, coming back with a steaming panful. Brett got up. "Go ahead. See what you can do with him, but don't poke nothin' into those holes."

When she was done Brett poured on more whisky. "Let's have them strips." Fastening a compress front and back, with her help he managed to get Trone tied up.

Looking up unexpectedly Brett found her watching him. He tried a smile for reassurance but guessed, even as he made the effort, it hadn't come out right. Her suspicion had blighted it, making him as conscious of himself as she had been. "I'll take him," Brett told her, lifting Trone in his arms. "Show me where."

She went ahead of him into the room the man had come out of. Brett saw the bed, the cigarette butts and bottles. She shook up the covers, got them out of the way, punched at the pillow. Brett put Trone down. He said, "I'll get his clothes off."

Brett stripped Trone to his underwear, long-handled, unbleached, and rank with sweat. He cut off the part the bullet had bloodied, pulled a blanket over the man and returned to the kitchen, dropping the fouled cloth into the stove.

The girl had washed and drawn a pan for him. Brett washed

with strong yellow soap, used the towel she reached out to him. He looked at her briefly and emptied the pan through an open window and put it back on the table. "I should of tied him up," Brett grumbled, thinking back to the kid.

She tried to hide her unease. "Wouldn't have made much difference."

Probably not. Short of beating hell out of the kid there wasn't much anyone could have done as things stood; no girl would want it told a man had tried. . . . Brett narrowed his eyes at her, knowing he'd got part of it. This girl, like himself, had a fight on her hands; something which, desperately hidden, incalculably frightening, wouldn't let her alone. Everything she did and saw and felt was colored by it. This was the difference, the unaccountable something which had caught at him. This was what had pulled him out here.

Sure, Brett thought, she was worried about Vic. But it went deeper than that, was more personal. It went beyond Trone's trouble. The girl put up a good front but deep inside her was this terror. It was the only word that would fit what Brett felt.

She started uncomfortably to thank him. Brett brushed the words aside. He wasn't comfortable himself, wondering if she'd understand his actions or purely hate him. In a way what he had done was inexcusable. Trone, like enough, would blow up and see red, might order him off the place, he thought sourly.

He got out his pipe and packed it and then stood with it in his hand, unlighted. "Your brother," he cleared his throat, "ain't in no shape right now for. . . . " This was going to be harder even than he had figured. "I better tell you what I've done," he said grimly. "They had a meetin' in town after you left. I've got no stake in this but I went—tole 'em I was reppin' for your brother. They voted him out of the Association, goin' to rebrand every Scab 8 they can find."

Eyes watching him darkly, she nodded.

He gave her a chance to speak her mind. When she didn't he

growled, "They'll be figurin' I'm out here account of my sister."

"Are you?"

Brett searched his thoughts. She had hard eyes to meet. "I don't think so." He thought some more and said carefully, "A man generally does what he figures he's got to. I ain't seen Jo in six years, if that means anything."

"Scab 8," she said, "isn't hiring guns."

The skin tightened a little around Brett's mouth. "Mine wouldn't be of much use if it was. I'm a horsebreaker, Lola."

"You know there's trouble shaping up. You know it's Hobbled O that's pushing it. Why did you come back?"

"I know there's trouble," Brett admitted. He found it hard to put his thoughts into words. "The trouble—well, it wasn't—I didn't know about you Trones. I don't know if I can tell this in a way that makes sense; I thought the trouble would probably be over me—expect it will, a good part of it." She wasn't giving him much help. He said, thinking how bald it sounded, "Not much of a recommend, is it?"

"Why did you feel you had to come to Packer's Crossing?"

He told her well as he could about his past, his reputation, about those things in his head that had persuaded him whatever he did would have to be done here.

"Where everything you touched went wrong? No," she said, looking straight into him, "that's not much of a recommendation."

He hadn't reached her. She could acknowledge her debt for what help he had given but her gratitude didn't extend to believing him. How could it? Would he have believed had their positions been reversed? The ranch, recorded half in his name; the wild things he'd done. She had good right not to trust him. Hell—Jo's brother! Would *any*one believe him?

He felt the heat in his cheeks. He turned away.

She said, "You must have seen what the range is like. Most of these people haven't got any water. This drought would finish all of us if she would just give it time."

Brett looked back at her over his shoulder. The girl might have read his mind. She asked, "Could anyone believe a man would go against his sister?"

"Probably not," Brett grunted. "They sure won't expect *me* to."

He stepped through the door but on the porch her voice stopped him. "They won't expect you to work for nothing. We haven't any money to spend on help but, if that's how you want it, put your stuff in the bunkhouse."

12

WHEN Rhode Island Red tore away from Scab 8 he had
only one impulse—to make good his escape. Before he had hardly
put Trone's buildings out of sight a second consideration anchored
all of his attention. Red had no false impression of where he stood
around Packer's Crossing; when word of this got out the whole
damned country might be after him.

Panic walled him off from rational thinking and, suddenly,
spurs were not enough. He began to flail the horse with his quirt.

Lather came through the wet dark of its coat, a rattle got into
the animal's breathing. The pounding hoofs faltered. Red flung a
twentieth look over his shoulder. Nothing in that vast stretch of
land moved behind him. Fright loosened its grip enough to let
other things catch his notice.

Resentment began to rise in him then, inspired by his recollection of Brett and his balked relations with Lola. The girl
wouldn't want that kind of thing known. She hadn't been hurt. It
might tie that fool's hands.

Then the scheme which had slipped Red's mind came back
and he stopped the staggering horse, sitting it there on braced legs
while the anger and spite and all the kill-hungry hate in him
swirled round his plan, considering the odds, pre-savoring the
heady aroma of triumph.

TICE chewed on the stump of a cold cigar, making no attempt to mask his dislike. This was the third dark after the ex-

pulsion of Trone at that meeting where Brett had slapped Tice around. Red had just ridden in, hadn't stopped at the house—enough in itself to have roused the segundo's suspicions; and the horse he'd got off of didn't belong to Hobbled O. Standing in the doorway of his quarters with the light streaming over his shoulders, Tice said, "Reckoned you'd pulled your picket pin," and considered the discolored bruise on Red's jaw, the torn dusty clothes and the strange horse behind him.

"Hoped's what you mean, ain't it? You going to keep me out here on this stoop all night?"

Tice reluctantly stepped aside and Red came through the door, shutting it back of him, leaning against it, some inner excitement prodding and pushing at him, leaching its shine through those pale winkless eyes, making his presence even harder to take. Tice, disquieted, shoved a chair out of his way and took up a stand where the light shone full in the kid's face.

"You got somethin' to say to me, say it an' get out," he growled. He'd never bothered, away from others, to conceal his dislike.

The kid, gingerly fingering his bruised jaw, grinned slyly. "Time you and me got together for a change."

"What's that supposed to mean?"

Red was trying to seem casual, confident of victory, but whatever it was he had bottled inside him wouldn't let him alone and the feel of this kept driving into Tice, nagging him like an aggravated tooth. "This thing's big enough for both of us," Red said.

"I ain't heard nothin' yet."

"I'll put it right in your lap. When I marry this spread you'll run it—"

"I'm runnin' it now—"

"Getting all you want, are you?" Red grinned wickedly. "I can pretty it up for you—if you want to string along. When Jo says 'I do' I'll see one third of the yield—after pay-offs—gets into your pockets. That's a lot of mazuma."

"By the looks of your mug I'd say you got a short memory."

Red's cheeks darkened, the coppery glint of his beard more pronounced. "I'm not forgetting anything. I can get along without you. I've as good as got this made right now. But you can help, make it easier maybe. You know cattle and grass; you can handle this crew. But you can't handle Jo or I wouldn't be here."

Tice said stiffly, "You spoke your piece?"

"I want it understood. There's a chance if we don't pull together in this we might not either of us get— He slapped you around, too."

Red took a moment then to pull his thoughts together, knowing Tice hadn't committed himself. He wouldn't have believed him if he had. All Red needed or cared about right now Tice would furnish without prodding, because it would feed his own poisons and just possibly raise his worth in Jo's eyes.

"Pee or get off the pot," Tice growled.

Red made up his mind. "I've been riding the hills up back of Trone's place. I can show you where there are seven Scab 8's that less than a week ago was packing our brand."

Tice eyed him, suddenly nodding. "Just tell me where they are," he said, "an' then keep your damn nose plumb out of it."

THIS same afternoon, a few hours earlier, a number of Trone's neighbors—other small owners—appeared at Scab 8 and were asked in by Trone's sister. Trone was up but not doing much, mostly sitting around, and when he saw who had come he dredged up a sour grin.

"We've been thinkin'," a skinny man said, fingering his hat.

When their host didn't help, this fellow said doggedly, "About them charges Tice flung at you—if he makes 'em stick there'll be no room here fer any of us. We've talked it over. We'll stand behind you."

Trone, finally getting up, went over to the stove and, rummaging in the box on the back of it, fished out a burnt match and returned. With the charred end he scratched a Hobbled O on the table top. Alongside of this he drew a replica of his own brand and brought his glance up slanchways. "You still standin' there?"

The brands looked like this:

O─O   Ô─Ô

Several of the men shifted around, eyes uneasy. The spokesman, Bud Lahr, flushing uncomfortably, said, "Hell—beggin' your pardon, ma'am—we know how easy it would be. We're not fools an' we don't figure you are. We don't think you done it."

"That touches me," Trone said, showing no sign of it. "What do you figure to do?"

"You wouldn't have much chance, all alone, if they come after you. Most of us ain't got much help around either but we thought, between the bunch of us, we could take turns stayin' over here, fix up some brush signals to bring the rest an' touch 'em off if. . . . You're lookin' kind of peaked, ain't you?"

"He's been sick," Lola said, and while the men stood looking at everything but one another and thinking naturally enough that he had been on the bottle, the hitched horses outside began to shift and through their lifted whinnyings came the sound of approaching hoofs.

Most of the men, faces tightening, stood trapped in their tracks. But Lahr, galvanized by his fears, sprang to the door with his gun coming almost unreached-for into his hand. His face went dark while they watched him; whirling he said with a plain suspicion, "What's *he* doin' here?"

Trone moved around one of the men and peered. "Breakin' some horse stock."

Lahr, bitterly waving his gun, almost exploded. "Brett Fasken! *By God, Vic, you're askin' for it!*"

They all wheeled around as Brett stepped on the porch. He

had seen the horses and knew Trone had company. He sat back on a porch rail, legs dangling, while the men, filing out, shouldered past without speaking. Lahr, filled with outrage, looked him straight in the eye.

Brett drawled, half grinning, "You fixin' to shoot somebody, Lahr, or just gettin' your steam up?"

Lahr had no humor. The question, and the whole look of Brett slammed down on top of it, affronted him considerably. He was a gangling six-footer with a pair of naturally protuberant eyes and a florid complexion that appeared at the moment to have a bad catch of sunburn. He rammed his gun into leather and without opening his mouth got onto his horse. Then, with his rein-wrapped hands above the horn, he glared back at Brett. "One of these high an' mighty days you Faskens are like to wake up on the road to hell!"

Brett's grin flashed again. "Just make sure you don't get in the way, Bud."

13

TRONE, with Lola back of him, stood in the door while the small-spreads bunch dribbled away from the place. The girl sighed, almost unconsciously, when the last of them had departed and her glance, coming around, touched Brett with a depth of misgiving that seemed more pronounced with each passing hour. As though, he thought sourly, the abrasive of his presence was chafing her insufferably. Perhaps it was the debt that lay so bleak between them.

Trone, eying Brett, said irritably, "Gad! You're about as popular as a breakin' out of smallpox."

"Ain't no law says you can't send me packin'."

"I keep rememberin' that."

Through an uncomfortable silence the two men watched each other, Fasken apparently indifferent, the rancher, gnawed by his doubts, openly edgy yet understandably reluctant. By the code of this land he was obligated to Brett; he had no other help, no further hope to lean on. Yet he could hardly bring himself to put reliance in the man. He had not asked Brett to come here, hadn't knowingly accepted one damned thing from him. But here he was, tough-faced and ungovernable, and maybe driving away the last chance Trone might have.

Brett could sense most of this in the way Trone was eying him. He put the flats of his hands on the rail, resettling himself, trying to resolve what was the right thing to do. The girl was afraid of him. Maybe Trone was too; the man was worried.

The look of Red came into Brett's thinking and all the planes of his face, grown somber, set bleakly. He believed he had gauged the situation, but nothing was following the moves he had figured to cope with. It was Tice he'd expected when he'd set out to come here; instead the kid had been already on tap and Trone down with a bullet. Nothing he'd foreseen was working out as he'd imagined. "If you don't want me here. . . ."

Trone, staring unfathomably, tramped off without comment.

Brett listened to the rancher moving about inside the house and sourly wondered if he'd gone to arm himself. There was a muted plop like a cow hauling out of a boghole, a peculiar stillness followed by a thump and the loudening clomp of Trone's boots returning.

He showed up in the door. "How many of those broncs you rode out?"

"Four you can count on. That dish-faced dun can use another couple saddles." Brett got out his tobacco. "What I just said was straight. You're not obliged to keep me. Those fellers—"

"Couldn't count on 'em anyway." Trone threw out a hand. "Flagler's the only real hope I ever had. You say he took up for me?"

"He's not going to help you. Not with my sister breathin' down his neck."

Trone sleeved sweat off his cheeks and quit the door. He took a place on the rail across from Brett, coming down on it in a way that told how much had gone out of him. He said, "It's not your sister that's botherin' me."

The girl went in. Brett glanced up with a sharpened interest. Jo could be rough when it made out to suit her. Trone nodded. "Might surprise you, Fasken, but she ain't runnin' that place—only thinks she is."

"Tice?" Brett packed his pipe.

"An' that kid. That damned Red."

Brett considered, scratched a match and fired up. "Expect you're wrong about that." He pushed the smoke away from him.

"Tice has been pantin' after Jo about as long as I can remember."

"Been some change around here since you been away."

"I'll lay they weren't brought about by somebody else."

Trone said flatly: "You sound pretty sure."

Brett considered this, wondering uneasily if he'd been taking too much for granted. People did change. Some ways. He'd changed himself, or liked to think he had. Clint Wilder's death might have hit Jo harder than he'd ever imagined.

He could see her as plain as though it had been just yesterday, cursing him, telling him she wouldn't have him round the place, that she never wanted to set eyes on him again. Throwing that wad of bills at him and himself stamping out of there like hell wouldn't have him. Maybe Clint's death. . . .

But it wouldn't have softened her. Tice and that kid might reckon as Trone did; Brett's views on the subject went back clean to childhood. Jo was pretty much like an Indian. It wasn't just selfishness or cussedness or greed. The kind of things that beat others only sharpened Jo's claws.

"Tell you somethin'," Brett said finally. "Better get some help around this place. You're goin'—"

"Takes hard cash to buy good whisky."

"Then you better lay off and put some coin where it's needed."

Lola came out while Trone was still glaring. "Something wrong?" she asked her brother.

She looked neat and clean in sun-bleached green print that tightly clung at breast and hip and likely influenced the heightened color with which her glance was drawn to Brett's.

She was, he thought, too conscious of herself, too serious about trifles no one else would have noticed, as though everything that touched her had an undersurface significance she must find and plumb. He wanted to shake her, even knowing her youth and lack of opportunities probably had as much to do with it as anything. It wasn't good for anyone to be all forted up like she was, watching the world from behind barricades. That business of Red hadn't helped her none. She'd hardly spoken to Brett since the feller had been here.

He pushed these thoughts away, caught by Trone's sharpened stare.

"Well?" Brett said thinly.

Trone's regard, narrower now, passed again between them and his cheeks darkened. "What the hell did you come here for?" The whole tone of it was ugly, rough-edged with suspicion. "You—"

"Don't reckon," Brett murmured, "I'd say that if I was you. Man holdin' a bunch of misbranded cattle should have a heap more to think about than proddin' up trouble."

Before the words were hardly out of Brett's mouth Trone was up off that rail. Lola's gasp cut between them. Her brother's eyes were a white blaze, the gun half out of his belt as the girl pushed a hand against his chest.

"Not callin' you a rustler," Brett said, never moving—"just giving you some facts to put your teeth in 'stead of that marmalade you been chewin'. There's seven Hobbled O steers and two cows up in them hills with your brand frooh burnt onto 'em."

"No!" the girl's voice was a stricken whisper.

Trone, now that Brett's talk had caught up with him, looked as though his eyes were going to roll off his cheekbones. He stood there, ludicrous, holding his gun. Mouth still open he spun, knees shaking, and was starting for the porch edge when Brett reached out and collared him. "What now?"

"I'm goin' after them cattle!" Trone snarled, twisting his head, the whole look of him crazy.

"You better sit down an' cool off. Last place you can afford to be jumped is with that stock." Brett let go of him and Trone came around. He looked rocky.

He had to swallow two or three times to get up enough spit to speak with. "Where—where are they?"

"You know that draw off east of the brush corral north of Oak Butte? They're up there, in that timber."

All of them now were still, wholly motionless, caught with the hard facts of how this would look and the probable consequences when and if that blotched stock was discovered by others.

"They'll be found," Brett said grimly—"only reason for 'em bein' there. Could be they're watched, but whether they're watched or not Hobbled O is goin' to know. It's my guess Tice will be ridin'. Once he gets to 'em he's got all the excuse he'll ever need for this business."

Lola said like she'd been running hard, "We've got to get them out of there!" but Brett shook his head. "And be caught with them?" The gold winked in his teeth. "That way you'll be finished about as quick as it takes to drop a rope over a limb. Up there that won't take hardly no time."

Trone's cheeks were gray, his eyes reminding Brett of a lynx he'd found in a trap one time, wild, gleaming with hate and frustration and fury. Some of the panic faded out of them. His jaw looked solid as a fist.

Brett put a hand against him, pushing him back. "And what's to become of Lola if you get yourself killed? This is a time to be thinkin', not goin' off half-cocked. There's a marshal at the Crossin'."

"Stoker!" A meanness was in Trone's voice. A kind of slow flush came over his sister's face. Her eyes fell away from Brett's, came darkly back. She said nervously, "What can we do?"

"He's got no rights here." That was Trone. "I told him once to keep off this ranch—"

"He's all the law there is," Brett said.

"Jo's law, bought an' paid for!"

Brett recalled Stoker from a long ways back, from before Trone had ever come into this country, and said quietly, "We've still got a little time, I figure. Tice'll want witnesses, more'n his own crew; likely try to get Flagler. He'll want him drawn into it. Anyhow it's Flagler he's got to impress. While he's shorin' that up you got a chance to go on record."

Trone backed away. His lips thinned and his eyes, wheeling over the yard, scoured the view like a hard-pushed bronc headed into a fence corner. "Not me," he growled. "I jest ain't in no shape for it."

"You want *I* should go?"

Trone, not meeting Brett's stare, shook his head. "Lola can ride in, if you think it's a thing that's got to be done."

"Look better," Brett said, "if you went yourself."

Trone's scowl got blacker. "I'm still runnin' this spread!"

Brett glanced at Lola. "I'll go change," she said. Her eyes came back to him. "Will you saddle up for me?" She went into the house without waiting for any reply.

"That's her hull," Trone pointed. He looked over at the corral. "Put it on that big chestnut."

"You ought to go yourself," Brett said again.

"You tryin' to run my neck into a noose?"

Brett held back the words that pushed against his teeth. The man had some right to his suspicions. "Someone," Brett said, "ought to ride to Hobbled O."

Trone stared thinly with his head tipped forward. "You'd like that, wouldn't you! You've done your part—what you come here to do; you've set it up for them—"

"Don't make yourself out a bigger fool than you are. Man with nothin' on his conscience, first thing he'd do—only *natural* thing, would be to get in touch with the owner of them cows. Maybe he wouldn't bother goin' to the law, but you're goin'. It's your only defense, without," Brett said, "you're figurin' to run."

"You think," Trone shouted, "I'd be fool enough to blotch them brands an' not have sense enough to—"

"I'm tryin' hard to believe somethin' but where there's all this smoke there's bound to be some fire. *Some*one's been gnawin' at these herds around here an' if you're caught with that stuff before you've showed good faith there ain't nobody goin' to stop to ask questions."

"All right—" Trone nodded grudgingly, "go tell her if you reckon it's worth all that ridin'." A ragged breath came out of him. "I been keepin' my end up any way I can—you don't know what it's like bein' alone like I been! Man that lives under the gun—"

Brett interrupted, fed up with him, "If you'd played this thing square—"

"Don't give me that!" Trone's eyes flashed like glass again. But his anger was smaller than the fears that were twisting him. "Look," he growled, coming bitterly toward Brett, "they'd take any excuse—you know it—to get me outa here! Alls I ever done is brand a handful of mavericks—stuff without a mark on 'em. How you figure your ol' man got his start?"

Some of the starch came out of him. He peered around nervously, head cocked to one side almost like he was listening. "We can't hold this place—"

"We'll hold it," Brett said.

Distrust came up out of Trone like a smell.

Brett looked at him bleakly then went across to the poles and got a rope off a saddle, snaked the chestnut out of the squealing pack and put the girl's rig on him, shaking the hump out of his gut, hauling the girth tight. One cinch was enough for a light rig like this, a California saddle; but when a man worked cows he'd damn well better have two, Texas fashion, if he didn't aim to come down over his mount's neck.

He stepped over to where he'd left his roan and screwed his own hull down. He led the animal to the trough and let him drink, stopping the process before the horse could take aboard enough to rattle in his bladder. Brett looked back across at Trone. "Got an extry rifle around here anyplace?"

"One in the barn," Trone grumbled, and Brett went over there thinking it a kind of odd place to keep a weapon. Not too peculiar though, everything considered. He found it leaning against a wall, just inside and to the left of the runway where a man would have it handy if he suddenly found the need.

He didn't hear the girl come in. He was standing there holding the black-powder Winchester, thinking about the thing; and when, to rid himself of this he turned, he walked right into her—might have knocked her down if he hadn't reached and grabbed her.

It was a natural thing, but he wasn't prepared for the reaction he got at the feel of her body shoved up against him that way or for the look on her face, her sudden stiffening. He didn't do anything—didn't even try, but some reflection of the thought must have reached her, for when he let her go she very nearly struck him. When she whirled, eyes too bright, to run out of the place, she was stopped in midstride by Brett's flat words: "You came in here for somethin'. Get it."

She had on a divided skirt, buff colored linen, snugly fitted at waist and thigh; a yellow scarf about the tightly buttoned collar of a faded turquoise shirt trimmed with ruffles down the front. He could see her agitation in the stiffness of her stance and the feeling that came out of her did not a thing to calm Brett.

She came around, narrowly watching; gauging her distance, she moved to pass him, Brett stepping back to give her room. But the combination of her distrust and the things so yeastily churning inside him made him put out an arm, catching hold of her shoulder. "You can't shut yourself up like a fly in a bottle! What's scarin' you's a part of every woman, Lola—a part of *bein'* a woman. It's rich and good; don't be ashamed of it."

Her face was still in the outside light but the shadow of her thoughts lay heavily across it. She was groping, still afraid of him, and her distrust was so strong it was almost rank. "There's nothing for you here," she said—"nothing! Do you understand?"

With a stifled sob she twisted free of him and ran.

14

BRETT shook his head, staring unseeingly at the light-streaked run of the barn's loose sheeting. Trone cursed his lot but it was Lola, buried out here and driven in upon herself with little knowledge and no experience, beset by imagination's phantoms, whose need held him here. It was herself the girl was so desperately afraid of, those inner drives and compulsions she could not understand and was unable to bring into line with her convictions.

She was gone when Brett came out with the rifle, the dust of her passage settling back over the ridge. Brett got into the saddle and reined the roan toward the hills that hid this part of Fasken range. When presently—for no sure reason—he glanced around, he found Trone watching from the open door.

He crossed the little hills. The sun dropped lower. The air was twisted and wriggly with heat, distorting whatever a man tried to look at, and smoky with haze where in the deeper distances the sky came down to brush baked earth. Brett's eyes seemed filled with ground glass or grit but there was no wind here, only this monstrous glare of heat that with unabating ferocity seemed to pour straight out of hell itself.

The grass underfoot in this light was gray. Seared and tough it gave off curls of dust, in some places so brittle the merest touch broke it, reducing it to chaff. Riding west across boundaries, staying away from the roads, it shouldn't be much over a four-hour trip. Plenty of time to see most of the things Brett would rather not look at—time enough, by God, to drive a man crazy, feeling the jaws of this thing closing in on him.

Just past dark he picked out the lights of Hobbled O, golden slashes in the blue-black immensity of unfathomable space. His father's ranch. . . .

No. Jo Fasken's ranch. He remembered the look of her the night he'd walked out with the money she'd flung at him fluttering about the harsh strike of his boots. She would never forgive him. No chance to start over—not for Brett Fasken, committed to keeping Trone's place out of her hands. And this on top of what he'd done to Clint Wilder.

She was like some great octopus, strangling this range, caring for nothing but power. Maybe killing Bill Tice and that kid wouldn't stop her, but it should whittle her down to where Flagler might.

A sobering thought. Brett considered it a long while, knowing that a few hours ago it wouldn't have occurred to him; shocked a little, too, at finding he had come in his thinking back to Flagler whose only real difference from Jo was a matter of degree—size and opportunity. They were cut from the same cloth. Flagler maybe wasn't as ruthless. He wasn't as far up the ladder, but it was just a matter of time, Brett thought sourly. And the man didn't have a great deal more than Trone had—time, that is; Trone and the other greasy-sackers in Jo's way.

The bunkhouse was dark. Two lamps still showed when Brett rode into the yard, both in the house. One of these, the farthest, behind a drawn shade, was in Brett's old room; the nearer was in what they'd always used for an office. Light from this ranged out across the dust, revealing the day pen open and empty.

So the crew was gone.

Most of Brett's time was in the bottom of the glass. Faces flittered unbidden through the corridors of his mind. Tice, molded by Jo's use of him, as intolerant as she was, ready to destroy anything in his path. Stoker, the marshal, slowed by the years, in debt to Jo for the only work he knew. The one-armed renegade, Schultz, warped by the fears that would not let him go. Flagler, caught in this Hobbled O trap with the rest of them, trying to figure which jump might put him on top. Clint Wilder, dead and probably laughing his head off. That goddam kid—that Rhode Island Red.

Brett pulled up by the gallery, wondering why he hadn't made Trone come with him. Scowling toward the office he got off his horse. A shivery coldness crept into him then as he listened to the silence and thought of that lamp at the other end of this place. The marshal's words came back: *He lives in the house an' nobody —not even Bill Tice—sets out to tell him what to do.*

I've been a fool, Brett thought, to come here without a gun.

No, this wasn't the time for that sort of thing. He'd been right. Trone's rifle was on the horse—he hadn't even thought to find if it was loaded! No matter. You didn't go into a house with a rifle to report stolen cattle and hope to convince anyone you'd come with clean hands. Violence grew its own kind of fruit—as who should know better than Brett Fasken!

He stepped onto the gallery and, withstanding the temptation to peer into the room, moved across to the door of the office and knocked.

The stillness became more intense. Then the whine of cicadas swelled into full chorus and against the shrill throb of this he heard the small sounds of feet approaching the door. He had suddenly a wild, almost desperate urge to run.

The door opened and Brett's sister was in front of him, against the light, little tendrils of hair fanned out round her head, silently surveying him, one hand still grasping the knob she had turned.

THE hand dropped.

"Come in," she said, stepping back to give him room. She walked around him to the desk and stood there, straight as he remembered, eying him without expression. "Shut the door," she said.

Brett heeled it to and put his back against it. She was still a handsome woman, but the years showed, every one of them. Probably because she'd just let herself go. The hard masculine traits she'd used to be at such pains to keep hidden were evident now.

She said before he could get his spiel going, "If you've come here to beg—"

"Don't you ever pull a comb through that hair any more?" Brett just couldn't help it. She could hit on more ways to get under his guard than a coiled tiger snake and he struck back—needing to hurt—just as he always had, without stopping to think. "Goin' round in pants! You tryin' to live up to that name they've hung on you?"

"Same old Brett," she said with her lip curled. "You're wasting your time. I said all I had to say to you before you left."

"I'm here," he said, "to report some blotched stuff we found that belongs to you. Packin' Trone's brand on top of Hobbled O, but he never put it there. I'm ridin' for Vic now. He sent me over to tell you—"

"There isn't anything you can tell me about that thief that will help him now. I've got him dead to rights—"

"He never touched those cows. He's been flat on his back in bed with a bullet."

She didn't believe him. She had made up her mind long ago about Trone. Peter and Paul—Jesus Christ himself—couldn't have held her back. She had Trone where she wanted him now. Brett had to say something. He said, "Stoker's been notified."

All that got him was a look of contempt. She was apparently thoroughly sure of the marshal. It riled Brett so fierce he said on a lunging outrush of breath, "You're ridin' for a fall! You're not going to get away with this!"

"You'd better go." She tipped back her head, still eying him, and spoke with a cold disdain. "That girl's turned your head. She's making a fool of you."

"Leave her out of this."

"My!" She canted her face at him. "You really are a fool. I'd think a man your age had been around enough to know a bitch in heat when he looked at one."

Brett was so furious he couldn't speak.

Jo laughed. "If you can't stand the truth the door's right behind you. Men!" she sneered. "I'm surprised you'd dare leave her long enough to come over here. From what I've heard—"

"Never mind what you've heard! You better be thinkin' what's going to happen if Currycomb gets into this. Flagler's no chump. He's not going to sit on his prat with his knees crossed while Tice and your outfit are puttin' the skids under him. You're like to wake up and find you've pushed yourself right plumb into hell. I'll tell you somethin' else—you got any regard for his health you better keep that kid away from me."

Her eyes went flat as fish scales. Her cheeks turned purple and then dead white. "You lay hand to that boy. . . . Get out! *Get out!*"

15

AFTER the sound of Brett's horse had faded Jo Fasken, cheeks mottled, collapsed into a chair. It wasn't too often a spell like this seized her but each one was harder; she had to fight for breath.

At last she fell back, spent and trembling. She knew Brett was right in what he'd said about Currycomb; she'd tried to tell Tice. That Flagler was holding still was no reason for assuming he would keep right on doing it. But you couldn't tell Tice anything.

Hobbled O—the brand—was Bill Tice's god. Backed by his crew of bleached-eyed Texicans his faith in the ranch transcended anything she had known. It was, to him, inconceivable any man or thing could stand against them. There were no boundaries to his faith, no shaking his bull-blind prejudice short of complete and irrevocable disaster.

Not that she imagined it would ever come to this. But just the same, things could get a little sticky if Flagler got his back up before Tice got the jump on those squatters. There'd be talk, regardless. God, how she hated the malicious backbiting of little minds, the only kind there were around here. Might even stir up an investigation. She'd been warned—almost begged—by the Governor. That pompous popinjay!

Maybe she should have listened to Red; he'd been after her to get rid of Tice. But Bill was just like a part of the business—she'd always had Bill to fall back on. People didn't argue with Tice, they shrank away from him, knees weak as water. He was something she had always been able to hold over them—habit—crowbar—

symbol of violence. Just the mere threat of him for years had been enough.

Now Brett was back and, no matter how it galled her, Brett was right about Currycomb. Flagler was no fool, and anything could happen with Brett mixed into this. He was one who'd never crawled for Tice, who had shown his contempt of the man even as a kid. . . . *Kid*.

The cold remembrance of Brett's words came back to set her shaking. He was perfectly capable. . . . The face of Clint Wilder wavered through her head, leaving her drenched in sweat, turning her half crazy. Wilder—according to Brett—was just a garden variety of snake. This opinion of his character had got back to Clint, or maybe Brett had come right out and told him to stay away from her. No one could rightly say how it started; there'd been a rip-roaring dinger of a fight in the Red Wall the night Brett left. Clint had jumped Brett, grabbing up a bottle—the whole town agreed on this. Brett had killed him, cracking Clint's head with a rung off a broken chair.

It could still make her violently ill, just the thought of it. She fought this nausea, knowing she had to get hold of herself. It was a time for action—something quick, sure, final.

She tramped the room in a fury of frustration, seething, breaking things. It was unthinkable Brett should interfere with her again—insufferable. She snatched up a vase and pitched it, swearing, through the window. There were ways. . . .

There'd been a kind of fascination about Clint Wilder, an excitement that had taken her to heights she'd never touched before. Red at best was pale beside him, lacking Clint's subtlety, Clint's capacity for evil. The kid could never fill the place left echoing inside her but he was all she had, her only pleasure. To think that once she could have had any man in this country!

It didn't pay to go looking back, the only profit was ahead. You took what you could, whatever you were able. This was none of Brett's concern. Red amused her; her enjoyment derived from observing his reactions to the mental pins she stuck in him. Red was her guinea pig. No one was going to take him away from her.

BRETT was in no better temper.

By all the signs there was like to be hell and no pitch hot. Jo had never taken a licking in her life except in the matter of that studhorse Wilder, and that deal had forced Brett out of the country. Well—not *forced* him maybe. But he'd gone all the same.

Damned if he was going to pull out again. Who the blue hell did she think she was! He rode two-three miles still fuming, cursing females in general and Jo in particular. *Mister Joseph*. Great Christ in the morning!

He kept thinking back to that scene, kept snorting, stewing, railing at the gall—the hateful arrogance of her. But deep in his bones Brett was mightily bothered. It was all well and good to talk but, come right down to it, what chance did he have any more than the rest of them? Jo had a habit of getting her way, a standing—Cod, how he hated that word!—to keep up, the prestige of Hobbled O, Joseph Fasken, and all the rest of it. And there was Tice to be reckoned with and Hobbled O's crew—not to mention Flagler and that brokle-faced killer.

A red-haired rat. That's what that kid was; but this didn't make the fact of him less dangerous. Even a goddam lizard could turn on you. A little rattler's bite was just as bad as a big one's—not that Brett was personally afraid of him. Not any more anyway than a man would be scared of any other kind of skunk. You didn't have to get soaked to know what it would do to you!

Brett did some hard thinking. You couldn't plan ahead very far. This deal was crammed with imponderables, shot with bogholes, riddled with impossibilities. There was nothing you could do about it. You took what came and that was the end of it.

Brett cut the roan into the north. A man might just as well get on with his work. It would take Lola a while to get here with

Stoker. They'd pick up fresh horses of course, maybe change a couple times, but it would sure be tomorrow and close to dark before they made it. Tice would show up first.

A lot would depend on Flagler, on how many of his outfit the Currycomb boss brought with him. Flagler might be pressured but he wouldn't be jumping into anything feet first. A man could talk to Flagler. He'd listen whether he did anything about it or not.

The corral where Brett had been working wasn't more than a mile and a half from the cows; he'd got onto them hearing them bawling for water. There was a windmill and tank at the corral and he'd fetched them back, knowing they'd return again when they got thirsty. He wasn't going to be caught riding herd on them but he aimed to be near enough to know when Tice found them.

It was about four o'clock when Brett reached the corral. The bluish starlight was dimmer but bright enough to show the horses still penned where he had left them, the unridden ones, the others he'd turned loose. They set up quite a racket.

He got down outside the gate. This was the kind of pen they built in New Mexico; Brett wondered if that was where Trone had hailed from. He pulled the rigging off Roanie, felt his feet and let him go, grinning as the horse folded into the dust, writhing around on his back, rolling three times then scrambling up to shake.

Brett went into the pen with hobbles and left the bars down when he came out, knowing the horses wouldn't get far before he wanted them. Finally he got his blanket—this being the coldest part of the night—and, picking up the rifle he'd got from Trone's barn, tiredly climbed a near ridge where he stretched out to get what sleep he could. He was thinking of Lola when at last it crept over him.

The sun, coming over the eastern rims, roused him. Or maybe it was the cattle. He got up and saw them coming, single-filing it in like Indians, the dust plopping up and rolling out—pretty near enveloping them—in ragged swirls like yellow smoke. He had figured they'd be in once they knew about this water.

He looked around for Trone's horses, spotting most of them without trouble. Two were out of sight, but he knew with those hobbles he would soon have them back again. Whistling for Roanie he shook out his blanket and picked up the rifle. Then he moved into the sharp-etched shadows of a clump of squatting cedars, giving the cows a chance to come in. They were plenty gaunt, real boneracks almost. Be no beef this year and damn little next if this drought didn't break almighty soon.

Roanie came up softly whickering. Brett rubbed his nose and let the horse nuzzle his pockets. When his nudgings turned a little rough with impatience Brett took out the plug of tobacco he kept for him and, breaking off a chunk, held it out, grinning as the roan shook his head up and down while he chewed. It was a kind of ritual with them and helped keep down the worms. Horse candy, Brett called it. He put the rest of it away and pushed the dark nose away from him. They'd been traveling together for about three years now. Brett had given seventy-five and wouldn't take a thousand dollars for him.

He looked off over the tank. There was no wind this morning. The air still was fresh but you could tell by the sky it was going to be another hot one. He hadn't thought to fetch anything along to eat, having figured to hit straight back from Hobbled O, and his stomach was beginning to remind him it was empty. He got out his pouch and packed his pipe and looked over the view. You couldn't see a hell of a ways around here. He watched the cattle trail off heading back for timber. What grass there was wasn't burnt near as bad up there but it was plain that Lola had known what she was talking about when she'd told Brett Jo didn't need to lift a finger. These small-spread outfits couldn't come through a dry like this. All Jo had to do was wait and pick up the pieces.

Someway his pipe didn't do him much good. He knocked it

out and put it away, grinding a heel on the coals before he straightened. "Well," he told Roanie, "guess we might's well get at it."

They went down to the tank. Brett splashed water into his face and rinsed his mouth out. He wasn't looking forward much to Hobbled O's arrival.

He put his saddle on the roan and slipped the bit between his teeth, more from habit than necessity. Roanie, an all-around cow horse, would work just as well without a damned thing on. They went hunting the pair that had got out of sight and found them off in the timber. Roanie pointed them back. Might's well start on them, Brett reckoned. He let Roanie haze one of the pair into the corral. He dropped his rope over the other, got down and put up the bars. Then he tied the roped one, snubbing him up short where the horse could see, not giving him enough slack to hurt himself. That was one thing about these cow horses, give them one good taste of the rope and they never forgot it.

The bronc in the pen was a loose-coupled, liver-colored bay with a star and snip. Brett, climbing into the pen, stood a few moments studying him, watching particularly his eyes and the way he placed his weight. "All right, feller, get your workin' clothes on. School's about to take up."

He went out and got his saddle, buckling a bar bit into his bridle in place of the cricket job he used with old Roanie. Brett was a man who was careful of a horse's mouth. Generally he preferred a hackamore but some horses—and this looked like one of them—needed something to get their teeth on and Brett wanted to keep all the toes he could.

Perching the saddle on the top pole of the gate he got the shorter length of cotton rope he'd bought at the store and slipped back inside the enclosure, the bay watching him suspiciously. Brett knotted a sliding loop in the rope, got it over the gelding's head and maneuvered him up to the post that was firmly set in the center of the pen. This was a typical Mexican breaking pen, round as a dollar, without any corners a horse could get into. He tied the bay to the post.

When he came up with the bridle the horse puts his ears back. Brett talked to him a while, held the leather out where he could smell of it. The horse jerked his head away.

When he could Brett liked to do this kind of work easy, taking his time with it, getting a horse used to each new thing as he went along. But he could see right away there'd be no point in it with this one; this bay was the kind that would never make up with you. He'd probably been started and spoiled. This was going to be a fight every jump of the way.

Brett dropped the bridle, grabbed the rope and snubbed the horse short. The animal's eyes rolled wickedly but there wasn't too much he could do, hobbled fore and aft and with that cotton rope cutting his wind off. Brett waited for him to ease up a little, promptly took in the slack and got that humped nose within a hand's length of the post. He tied him there and went back for his blanket.

The horse couldn't kick and after a couple of tentative tries seemed to be smart enough to know it. He watched Brett balefully, flinching and trembling when Brett put the blanket on. Brett got an arm over his neck, manhandled the bit into his mouth and secured the bridle. He came up with the saddle, settled it back of the withers, kneed the wind out of the bronc, took up on the strap, thumped him again in the gut, took up two more inches and tucked in the end.

It was getting warm.

Stepping back, Brett passed a glance over the landscape. No sign yet of Tice. Brett climbed out and got a drink from the tank, sleeving the excess off his chin, hearing the bristles scrape. Hell of a job for this kind of weather.

Brett grunted, looked around again and got back into the

pen. He tied his neckerchief over the bay's rolling eyes, jerked off the hobbles, untied the free end of the rope from the post and put a foot in the stirrup.

The bay, still trembling, stood like a rock.

Brett wrapped the freed end of the rope round the horn, took a good solid hold and went up. The horse kind of squatted but stayed in its tracks, ears back, filled with tension. Brett peered around for a good place to land. He was glad he'd remembered to leave the rifle outside. He jerked off the blind.

The horse felt to Brett like a stack of bunched springs. Suddenly his head came around, teeth bared. Brett struck him across the nose with the rein ends. When he still tried to reach, Brett put a fist between his ears. The brute's head went down, his hind end came up as though an explosion had lifted it. Brett grabbed with his knees and the fight was on.

This Roman-nosed bay was an expert. There wasn't anything Brett knew that the horse didn't try. He pitched, plain and fancy. He bucked for ten jumps in one spot then viciously swapped ends. He twisted and reared, seemed about to throw himself backward and, when Brett failed to buy this, started fence-worming, leaving the ground in one direction and coming down hard in another. Brett could feel blood getting into his nose but stayed put.

The bay cloud-hunted. He bucked in circles and figure eights. He tried shaking and weaving. He did a spot of pioneering. He went into a crescent, sunfishing, striking right and left, as if trying to touch the ground with one shoulder and then the other, letting the sunlight flash against his belly. Then he started pile-driving, humping his back, coming down with all four legs stiff as fence posts. Brett felt like his spine was going to go through his hat. There was so damned much dust you couldn't see anything. The horse went into a double shuffle, jackknifed, went up into a spin. Just when Brett had about made up his mind he couldn't last another jump the horse quit to stand head down, sides heaving. Brett just sat there, too pooped to get off.

16

ON the night before—at about the time Brett first saw the lights of the Fasken ranch—a quite different atmosphere held sway in the office from the quiet Brett found when he stepped in three quarters of an hour later.

Jo Fasken, then, hadn't been alone. Bill Tice was there— very much so, in fact. He had one of his men in the doorway back of him, a breed called Mora, a thin slash of a man who packed two guns and wasn't finicky about using them.

Jo got a glass from a drawer and pushed a bottle across the desk. "Help yourself."

Tice poured a stiff slug and tossed it into him, nodding. He stood then with lips drawn back and said, "We've got him!" some of the excitement cooped up inside him spilling out with the words and setting up little trembles of agitated air. "Got him dead to rights!"

"Perhaps," Jo said dryly, "I could come nearer sharing your congratulations if I had some idea what you're talking about."

"Trone." Tice grinned. "Found a dozen of our critters up near Oak Butte cached away in a draw with his brand worked over them."

She didn't speak straight off but sat a while considering. "All right. That's plain enough. What do you propose to do?"

It was Tice's turn to weigh things. The burly range boss eyed her carefully. He generally figured to pretty well understand what was back of her remarks, but when she got that look on her face a man might just as well stare at a cactus.

Tice snorted impatiently. "Hang 'im—what else! Ain't that what we been wantin'?"

"Better take Flagler along."

"Sure." Tice stared. "He'll have his paws on the rope." He could have told her this had been his plan from the first. But sometimes it was handy—if things didn't exactly work out as figured—not to have all the credit. Tice said now with an ironic politeness, "Anythin' else frettin'?"

Her eyes stared back, black as malpais. "Split that range up with Flagler. See that he gets his share of Trone's cows." Her eyes kept prodding. "That's an order. Never hurts, Bill, to soften a man up a little."

Color flooded up from Tice's collar, turning darker as it rose. "I never saw the man I couldn't handle," he said flatly.

"Never mind. Do it my way."

Tice shoved Mora into the yard and tramped after him.

The kid—Rhode Island Red—pushed through another door, pleased by the affronted temper that had bristled in Tice's parting words. He was careful, however, not to let Brett's sister see this. He pulled out a chair and straddled it, resting his arms across the back and trying to ignore the rankling cut of Jo's stare.

"You're like to lose an ear sometime doing that."

Red grinned, inflated with new confidence by the knowledge that was in him. "Hell," he said brashly, "I'm the feller found those steers."

Some of the cockiness leached out of him then and he said in a tone that was propped up with bluster, "Hadn't been for me you'd still be going round in circles."

"Four nights." Her eyes dug harder. "Where have you been?"

"Just riding around. Country's going to blow away if this keeps up much longer." Then he said, hoping to change the subject, "When we fixing to get married, Jo?"

"What's that bruise on your face?"

This was where Brett had hit him. "Damn horse spooked—whacked me into a tree limb. We going to throw a real jamboree—"

"We're not throwing anything till this business is over."

Red's eyes turned sullen. "I'm getting plenty fed up with playing lap dog around here."

"Think you're up to running this ranch?"

"Tice can do that. It's what he gets paid for."

"You're doing all right."

"For a fifth wheel, sure." Red's temper got away from him. "You think I like people sniggerin' behind my back? I got feelings, by God!" He almost shouted it at her, remembering just in time to drag his voice down but unable to get the ugliness out of it. "I don't have to be just a convenience to *any*one. I know *some* that would give their last dime for my talents."

He stepped away from his chair with an unhideable nervousness, not liking at all that bleak shine in her look. But the damage was done and he didn't know how to undo it. A flare of defiance sent more words tumbling out of him. "I could get me a deal from any of that crowd—Flagler, too!"

Still-faced, she nodded. "That what you want to do? Go out and kill somebody?"

Suspecting mockery, he scowled. "I could do that too!" Her look kept bothering him, aggravating his temper and at the same time, someway, inexplicably disquieting him. He slatted a look over his shoulder half expecting to see Tice, but there was no one.

He dragged his tongue across dry lips, suddenly afraid without knowing what was gnawing him. He backed away in the direction of the door he had come in by. His groping hand found the knob and breath rushed into his chest again. He'd be a fool to duck out with no more than he'd brought into this; a fool twice over if he ran empty-handed after the risk he'd taken in the matter of those cattle.

Pride wouldn't let him withdraw what he had said and his fears and greed, stirred up and flogged by his ambition, wouldn't let him play the mouse without at least one final try at it. Assuming a bravado he was far from feeling he tossed out his ultimatum, "I don't *have* to go to Flagler—it's up to you. But I ain't going to risk it for any sackful of peanuts! Blood's going to be spilt and if I string along I've got to see some of the gravy. There's a J. P. at Packer's. All you'd have to do is ride in with me."

Sweat shone on his cheeks. She eyed him so long he began to get panicky. Hoofs rumbled over the yard—the crew departing. Somewhere a coyote yapped, sawing at Red's nerve ends, deepening his alarm, his growing sense of isolation. His grip tightened on the knob. "Why don't you say something!"

She was watching him inscrutably. A corner of her mouth lifted. "You really are fond of me, aren't you?"

"Of course—'course I am!" It was too loud, too quick, too emphatic. His goddam voice got clean away from him. Numb with shock he heard himself yell like a bleating idiot. Something had touched him, brushed against his shoulder. He spun like a cat, ripping the gun from his armpit, hammer lifting. But it was only a coat hung on the back of the door.

Jo's mouth twitched again.

"I'll think about it," she said.

"You got till tomorrow night," Red snarled, and yanked open the door, slamming it back of him.

Even through the planks he heard the sound of her laughter. She didn't think he'd leave her, didn't think he'd dare to! She didn't look to have any trouble but by God she would have! *Just you wait*, he thought viciously. She'd be mighty quick glad to take him on any terms, anything to keep him on her side and away from Flagler—*he'd build a fire under her!*

He got an old felt hat from his room and shrugged into a brush jacket, went around the back way and slipped a horse from the corral. Half an hour later, out of sight and sound of the house, he pointed the animal toward the peaks of the Glories and drove in the spurs. Ollie Schultz didn't know it but he was a dead man right then.

17

BRETT, with three of the rough string ridden, was more than half in a mood by the middle of the morning to finish out the dun he'd told Trone about and call it a day. It was grueling work under the best of conditions, and in this kind of weather it was damn near murder. He sank back against the poles, soaked with sweat, breath wheezing, fatigue so deep in his bones he was shaking.

His mind was numb from the pounding he had taken, every movement a misery, every breath a burning anguish. The old wound in his leg was filled with fire but he finally limped over to the tank and, flat on his belly, soaked his throbbing head. He felt enough restored after a while to get up and cuff a little of the dust from his grimy clothes. He took another look around, wondering what was keeping Tice. He should have been here by this time.

He eyed the ridges again, staring long toward the timber. He could comprehend their not coming while darkness remained—Flagler, at least, having too much savvy to risk riding into any chance of an ambush; but it had been light for six hours. Shouldn't take more than three to get here from Currycomb.

Brett didn't think Tice would show without Flagler. Tice and Jo would want Currycomb neck deep in this for the looks of the thing if for no other reason. And, if Brett knew his sister, the spoils would be split right down the middle, half Trone's grass and half his cattle going to Currycomb; this was politics.

Maybe Flagler had refused to have anything to do with it. Didn't seem too likely. Flagler had his end to keep up. No matter how reluctant the man might be, self-interest would exert a considerable pressure and there could be no neutrality. He had to string with Hobbled O or make a deal with the small spreads. From what Brett had seen and heard the night Tice had gotten Trone thrown out of the Association, there didn't seem but one course Flagler could follow. There was always hope of some amicable settlement and Flagler wouldn't be the first to be left holding that illusion. Nobody with a lick of sense would set out to buck an outfit like Fasken ranch if they had any choice at all.

Which was why big outfits got bigger, Brett decided disgustedly.

His worries piled up, magnifying themselves. Wouldn't be too much sound away off there even to start with and, riding like he'd been, he mightn't have heard it if there had been. He was half of a mind to ride over to that draw and find out right now if Tice had been around. He even started for his horse, saddle in hand, then hooted himself out of it. *Keep on like this and you'll be jumpin' at gophers!*

He crawled into the pen through the poles with his saddle.

TRONE, at Scab 8, put in a bad night. He had finally drunk himself into a stupor, but this was so normal a part of his routine that he was up by eight, bumbling around with his bloodshot stare, knocking holes in the tops of several tins of tomatoes. This helped, but not enough, so he brewed up a great scalding pot of black coffee, casting back over the past in his mind while he drank it. That slug the kid had put into him had stirred up a number of things he would sooner have left forgotten.

He'd been raised strict—him and Lola both—by God-fearing parents who'd believed hard work was the answer to pretty near everything—hard work and prayer. Vic had never been long on patience and sure as hell hadn't aimed to end up a dull boy. When he got big enough he'd thrashed the old man and taken off one dark night with all the cash on hand, determined to get out of life what he felt like.

Fed to the gills with established virtues he'd sought easier pickings and had not infrequently found them in the company of kindred spirits. He had the world's tail plumb wrapped round his saddlehorn: whisky and women and cards and all the rest of it, but nothing too serious till he'd got into that bank heist. That was the belly blow. Three men had been killed, including both his companions, and the job hadn't yielded one stinking penny. Kansas, that was—he'd put all his luck down the drain getting clear. He finally made it into Colorado, so goddam scared he could still get the shakes just thinking about it.

He'd forsook most of his wilder ways and gone to punching cattle, but the Pinkertons were strong on keeping old scores alive. They'd never crossed that job off their books and one day Vic's boss had asked him point black where he'd come from. Seemed some feller was asking around about a gent that pretty generally fitted Trone's description. Vic hadn't asked for any further particulars. He'd thrown his hull on a hide and got the hell out of there. That was the year his mother had died.

The passing of Vic's dad the following spring had finally taken Trone back to look up the sister he'd scarcely more than remembered. He'd been considerably astonished to discover the old man had been pretty well fixed. Everything had been left to Lola; and Vic—quite engaging when he bothered to go to the effort—hadn't had much trouble persuading her there was more to be made out of ranching these days. They'd sold the farm and bought up a bunch of cattle, but it had been a little more difficult finding good range a man could get a toehold on. They got out of Nebraska and tried Texas and New Mexico, both too late.

Here under the shadow of the Glories—the Galiuro Mountains —in southeastern Arizona Territory they had taken the final plunge. Vic's hard luck stuck with him like a burr. Rustlers plagued him, and their two hands quit, intimidated. Hobbled O shut off his credit. He got another hand with a lot of reckless promises then lost him to unknown snipers. The drought came on. Rustlers hit him. He got to drinking heavy again.

Because he was still in mortal terror of being tagged with that old bank rap he'd made no local alliances, keeping away from things, making recluses of both of them. Continuing rustler depredations on top of the long drought became more than Vic could take. He struck back by slapping his brand on every maverick he could come up with. Like he told Brett, plenty of gents had got set up in this fashion. But in those days there hadn't been any law against it. Now there was and, while putting your mark on unbranded stuff wasn't deemed bad enough to call for a lynch rope, they put you away for a good stiff while. But Tice wasn't interested in just putting him away.

In Vic's kind of fix you simply had to trust someone, and after a great deal of wavering Trone had made up his mind to string with Fasken. He sure as hell didn't want to, but that had nothing to do with it. Tice had framed him and Tice, if he got hold of him, would hang Vic sure as God made apples. Vic didn't aim to sit around here and wait for it!

This was where the trust came in. Brett would stay on if she asked him—he was that kind of fool. Not even Brett, however—tough as Brett was—could keep Lola going without Vic could manage—and he felt pretty sure he could—to make some deal with the law whereby Scab 8 could be a legitimate spread again.

Stoker was the key as Vic saw it. The marshal, though he'd never spoke, was as gone on Lola as a man could be, plumb worshiping the ground she walked on. Even more important to Vic's calculations, the man never figured he had any chance. Vic could tell him real fervent and private that if Stoker, as marshal, would give Scab 8 his best efforts he—Vic Trone—would make a full confession of the stuff he had mavericked and stay out of Stoker's way if Syd wanted to sit the bag for her. That, plus Fasken, should take care of Lola and he could go off with a free mind to serve whatever time he had coming.

The only hitch that occurred to Vic's mind was the possibility —once they got him in prison—of the law catching up with that old bank business. But this didn't seem too likely. Yuma was a hell of a long ways from Kansas and not even the Pinkertons would look to find him in prison.

Might be a good idea, it suddenly struck him, to get away from this place while he still had the chance. He lifted down the rifle that was over the antlers in the sitting room, tugged down the brim of his hat and stepped into the smash of the midmorning sun.

Bitterly cursing the heat he was halfway across the burning dust of the yard, heading for the horse trap, when the sound of approaching hoofs spun him around with a lift of panic. It was too soon for Stoker—too late for flight.

He was half ringed by the shapes of waiting men, caught flat-footed in the glint of their weapons.

18

HAVING put another ride on the dun and taken him through a second brief course in reining—very different in application from that given eastern stock—Brett, while he had the time and inclination, reckoned he might just as well take the bronc a step further. Picking up an old burlap he'd found kicking around he sacked the horse out, flapping it at him while holding him snubbed, snapping his chest and belly and legs with it, dragging it over the tail-tucked rump until the dun at last stood with scarcely a quiver. Jerking his saddle Brett turned the horse loose.

Standing back in the hot yellow shadow of the pen Brett watched the dun go plunging away, slide into a trot half circling the place and come swinging back toward the tank to stand blowing above the water, still bunched and warily canted, ready to take off if it appeared Brett wasn't done with him.

Finally the horse dropped his head, lipping the water, pushing his nose through it. Brett turned away, creaky as a poortown gate hinge, clothes plastered to him at crotch and chest, bound tight with sweat across the bulge of his shoulders. He hauled the tails of his shirt out, flapping them, trying to stir up a little air. He knuckled the smart of his sweat-inflamed eyes and whistled up Roanie.

He picked up his blanket and settled it back of the withers —hair side out to keep the dampness from galling—and cinched down his hull, slipping the bridle over that chocolate head, pushing the bit into place, grumbling, worrying. He got the rifle Trone had loaned him, blew the dust out and tried the action. He slid

94

the barrel into the scabbard that was under the left fender and pushed out his cheeks and got aboard, still scowling, looking back at the dun but not worried about him. No range-bred horse was going to founder himself. It was Trone that was turning Brett's thinking so jumpy—Tice, Flagler and company.

He kneed the roan into motion, bound for the draw where the cattle had been browsing, faced with the need of quieting his own fears.

That bunch should have been here at least two hours ago— he peered disgustedly overhead. Damn near noon! A kind of grimness appeared to settle into him more deeply as he directed dark looks across the rims of the ridgetops. It went against all his precepts to be found near those cattle, but if Tice and his outfit had been by Brett needed to know it, and if they hadn't it was time he made some effort to find out why.

He rode carefully, quietly. No cattle in the draw, none visible in the timber—no rope fruit dangling from any of the branches. But Tice had been here; anyways someone had. Tracks all over. He got down on his haunches and studied a few of them; picked up some horse droppings, mealing them through his fingers, wiping his hands in the dust, weighing the situation. Three-four hours ago; likely a dozen of them. The cattle had been drifted together, eased off into the west toward Hobbled O head-quarters, two riders trailing. The rest of the outfit had gone on toward Trone's.

And the marshal not due until just about dusk. Sure, he'd reach the ranch sooner, but not soon enough if Trone had been there when these fellers showed.

Brett could feel it narrowing in on him.

No trouble following the tracks. This bunch had a start of well over three hours, time enough to get there and be on the way back. Brett rode steadily. No point in hurrying. Practical to get straight out of the country. He wooled it around a while, never having for a moment the least intention of clearing out. Couldn't blame a man much for wanting to, though. Brett was stubborn. He admitted it. But this wasn't just contrariness.

It was nearing two when he sighted dust. He kept right on, more watchful now, his eyes coal-black between the cracks of his lids. He neither swerved nor pulled rein when a muddle of horse-backers crested a ridge, suddenly stopping. They'd seen him, all right; likely recognized him too. He had no bother making out Tice and Flagler. They were coming on now, quickly closing the distance. He heard the pound of their hoofs, the outflung echo of Flagler's shout.

Brett slid the Winchester out of its scabbard, riding with it cradled across his thighs. He could probably outrun them if he were put to it. He'd no way of knowing what they'd found back at Trone's, but if Vic had been there. . . . He didn't follow this thought. He stopped his horse on the flat. He said, "That's far enough," when they came into long handgun range. "Right like you are."

Tice began yelling for a rope. There was some shifting amongst them that stirred up more dust and two men along the edges started to edge out a little but changed their minds when they caught Brett's look. Brett felt the keyed-up tension of Flagler's stare, saw small signs of nervousness in one or two of the others. Most of the dust settled. "You always did talk pretty large," Tice said. "Get off that horse."

The gold in Brett's teeth flashed. The nearest man edged away from Tice.

Tice said, "You had your warnin'." An ugly satisfaction pushed into his face. "I told you how this was goin' to be. Now get off that horse!"

One of Brett's hands still held the Winchester's barrel across the roan's neck; there'd be a lift of several inches if he intended to use it. His legs were straight down in the stirrups, shoulders a little hunched, elbows out. He held Tice's stare, neither moving nor speaking.

They were about of a size, Brett maybe ten years younger, more to be feared in a rough-and-tumble but slower, less likely to get off a shot if this ended in fireworks. You could almost watch these thoughts going through Tice. He loosed a passionate yell. "Get down! Get down!"

"You need all this help, Bill?"

"Flagler—" Tice yelled in a half-strangled voice, "put your rope on him!"

The Currycomb boss sat as though he were glued there.

"I don't think," Brett drawled, "he's that much of a chump. No rope ever twisted is goin' to outrace a bullet."

This was making Tice look silly, turning him wild but not wild enough to let himself go completely. He put a hand against his hip and was teetering on the edge of it when Brett said clearly, "You might get me but you're not going to have long to brag about it," and his knee brought the shoulder of the roan around so that Tice found himself staring into the rifle's muzzle. "You can drop that pistol or pull it," Brett said, "but you better be doin' either one or the other. I'll count just so far."

He said, "One." He said, "Two," very clearly in that quiet. With a ragged shout Tice let go of the half-out Colt, his hand springing from it as though the gun were stove hot. Somewhere inside the man something shattered. Shame rushed into his twisted cheeks. His eyes rolled like a stallion bronc's. There was a bitterness in him that would not let him stay still and his voice came out in a furious shout: "You're a mad dog, Fasken—I'm goin' to drop you on sight! Them's the orders my men'll have! Don't let another sun find you here!"

"So long," Brett sighed, and watched them pull around him, kicking tired horses into a run.

He had guessed that when the chips were really down and it came to trading lives Tice would not be up to it. The man had traveled too long on reputation. He hadn't been called and he was rusty and Brett's bluff had caught him short.

Brett was shaking at the knees, drenched with sweat, not sure himself even now if he would have had the guts to go through with a shoot-out if Tice hadn't cracked. There were no false hopes buoying Brett. Tice's failure to go through with this would set the man crazy—he would never rest until Brett was dead. That made two of them, Tice and that kid. Two of them gunning for him, and the Hobbled O crew. Sworn to shoot on sight.

IT was crowding four when Brett rode into the ranch. A furnace wind had whipped up over the last two-three miles, chasing tatters of dust clean across the horizon. Grit stung Brett's cheeks. His eyes were streaming. As the roan, shouldering these gusts, moved into the yard Brett fleetingly reckoned he must have been loco ever to have dreamed he could start over here. It was kill or be killed if he stayed any longer.

His mouth folded bleakly when the horse, jumping sideways, arched his back at a huddled shape.

Brett quieted the horse and got out of the saddle, letting go of the reins. He didn't touch Trone, didn't go any closer, stood there staring for an interminable while. He saw the blood and the rifle, the tracks of milling horses.

He turned at last, moving toward the house, warned by the slant of the swaying, partly open, half-askew door, but going on anyway, wanting to see with his own eyes what they'd done. One glance inside from the porch was enough.

He hadn't realized he'd fetched the Winchester from his saddle till he sat down on the step and put the rifle across his knees.

19

THIS was where they found him, Trone's sister and the marshal, when they came in on blowing horses some fifty minutes later.

Pulling up near the pens Stoker motioned the girl to stay where she was and swung stiffly down, reading signs as he went, approaching Trone's shape much as Brett had done to stand grimly silent, chewing the fringe of his moustache, looking as though his worst fears had been realized. Lola came up and with blanched cheeks turned her head to stare unreadably at Brett.

The marshal, finally stirring, went over and picked up Trone's unfired rifle, wiping some of the dust off, examining it without comment. He was an old man suddenly in a job that had got too big for him. It showed in the way he stood there, in the hopeless way his worried glance swept the yard.

Brett, still gripping the Winchester, stood up as Lola, followed by Stoker, came over to the porch. She looked as though she were walking in her sleep. The marshal growled, "You didn't see it?"

Brett slanched him a thin look and shook his head. He mentioned his trip to Hobbled O, just roughing it in, explained about the horses and then said flatly, "No matter which one of them brought him down—and it looks like they all had their irons out of leather—Tice and Flagler were leadin' that bunch. Look in the house. You never saw nothing like it."

Stoker, obviously reluctant, stepped up onto the porch. He pushed back the broken door, went in and tramped around and came out chewing his lip. There was a grayly hollow look about the man that made Brett say, "Well? Looks like you got to get off the fence."

Stoker gave him a bitter stare.

"Maybe," Brett said, "that wasn't called for. Still your move."

"What do you think I better do?"

"I know what you *ought* to do. You ought to lock them up."

Stoker said testily, "I'm only a town marshal. You're talkin' sheriff's business. Even if I had jurisdiction it would be your word against theirs. Two most influential cowmen around here."

"You're goin' to let them get away with this?"

"Be reasonable, man!" Stoker cried at him irritably. "Put yourself in my place—you think they'd hold still for that? I'd never get out of their yards with those two—"

"Deputize me. I'll bring 'em in."

Stoker said without preamble, "You're under arrest."

Brett said, "Are you foolin'?" He didn't move but his eyes bit into the badge-toter blackly.

Stoker glared back at him. "Schultz was shot last night—Ollie Schultz. Killed right on his doorstep—"

"And Trone was killed right here in this yard. In broad daylight," Brett said, "and you can't touch it!"

The marshal flushed. "Not the same thing at all! Trone's been outlawed; all I got is your word, yours against theirs, and no witnesses." He peered at Brett. "I mind how it was in the old days," he grumbled. "Up pops Brett Fasken and just like that you got trouble." He shook his head irritably. "Bud Lahr rode in—"

"Lahr hates my guts!"

"Lahr's not accusin' you. He fetched a signed statement from Ollie's wife namin' you—"

"Never seen the woman."

"Ollie must've identified you. She claims you rode up right after they'd lit the lamps. Says you called Ollie out and shot him. Just called him out and shot him," Stoker growled. "He didn't even have a gun on him."

Brett stared darkly. Trone hadn't fired his. "Right about then I was. . . ." He let the rest go, knowing the futility of anything he might say. Talk wasn't going to help; they were past talk. That day in the Mercantile at Packer's Crossing, in front of Syd Stoker, Schultz's terror had sown the seeds of this. Likely told his wife about it. Ollie with a guilty conscience about that water he'd fenced off had been scared half to death of Brett. If the lamps had been lit and it happened the way Stoker told it Schultz couldn't have seen anything, but he could have called out Brett's name. It was Brett that had put his wind up—Brett coming back and all this trouble cropping up.

Brett considered the marshal wearily. "If you're out of your bailwick for Tice and Flagler—"

"That's right. Off my range. No authority at all. Just reckoned you probably better know about Schultz." He regarded the bone buttons of Brett's salt-rimed shirt. "If Trone'd been alive I might of done somethin'—aimed to." He made a querulous shift of one arm, eying Lola. He wiped sweat out of his wrinkles and, setting Trone's gun against a post, squared his shoulders, again peering at Brett. "Nothin' personal, understand, but if I should see you in town I'll have to take you."

Brett didn't answer. The marshal, facing Lola, took off his hat. "You better come along an' stay a spell at the Crossin'. I could sort of keep an eye out—better anyway. You can't stay here."

The girl, ignoring him, was still watching Brett. "That's right," Brett said. "Bound to get rougher 'fore it gets any better. You go on in to town. I'll watch the place."

"I'm not going anywhere."

Stoker's breath weaseled out in a kind of long sigh. He put on his hat and tramped across the dust and got into his saddle and put the horse about. He wasn't old in years but he was feeling every one of them.

In a way Brett, watching him out of sight, felt sorry for him. Fifty wasn't too old for a man to think about a woman. He could tell by Lola's face most of the shock had worn away. What she needed right now was a good hard cry and going into that house would likely take care of it.

Brett got his blanket off the corral and covered Trone to keep the flies off. He went to the barn to find a shovel.

No use blaming Stoker. He'd been conditioned too long to seeing Tice have his way. Syd owed his star to Jo but some things he would do, regardless. He couldn't swallow Brett's story about wanting a fresh start. In the marshal's book Brett was here because Jo had sent for him and, up to a point, Syd would go along with that. But if Brett came into town Stoker would take him or go down trying. No one but a fool would stick with this any longer. What good would it do? He couldn't buck the whole country!

All the while Brett was digging his thoughts plunged uncontrollably on, round and around, trying to find some fissure of hope, some way he might yet pull a measure of security out of this mess for Trone's sister. There didn't look to be a chance and the knowledge lay sour in his belly that only a gun could finish some kinds of trouble, that no gun would be doing this in the hands of Brett Fasken.

He stared down at them bitterly—strong, big, capable hands, as useless in this deal as bloomers on a heifer. That kid—Bill Tice certainly, and probably even Syd Stoker, could shoot circles around him, cut him into doll rags. And two of them sure as hell would try. Just the sheer weight of numbers. . . .

He stood suddenly still, intently staring. *The sheer weight of numbers.* But only two or three people—four at most—pulled the strings. Tice, Rhode Island Red, Flagler maybe, and Stoker by the grace of Jo Fasken and that badge. They were all being kept in motion by Brett's sister. She was the point around which they revolved.

A rock. But with luck a man might work on those others, spook or maneuver them to where, one by one. . . . A fine thought.

Might be something to it if a man could shove a gun up against them, but there it was. Back to guns.

It just wasn't good enough. Brett amended that. *He* wasn't.

He went on with his work. When he reckoned the hole was sufficiently deep he started back to the house but, just short of the porch, sheered off toward the barn. No point making this any harder than it was for her.

He fetched a tarp and rolled Trone in it. He would like to have given him a full-rig funeral; might have shaken some people to see Vic laid out with all those bullet holes. Might have made them think a little, take a sharper look at what this country was headed for.

The weather was against it. Carrying Trone over to the hole he cased him in.

Brett, pulling off his hat, stood a while in silence with the sweat running off him and, over in the cottonwoods, a mockingbird retching up a steady beat of sound. In this kind of game a man wasn't dealing in wishes or theories but with the cold hard facts of power politics. Jo had lived so long in a world of her own she couldn't bring herself to share even a piece of the scenery without she could dictate terms of tenure. She wanted it all, every last shovelful. And then she would probably squeeze it for more.

Flagler, on a lesser scale, was out of the same mold. Not as bold or big, not as ruthless maybe, but just as much a pirate within the limit of his opportunities. He was bound in the same direction and he wasn't going to make it—even *he* must sense that now. Jo had outflanked him, involving him with Trone. His hands were legally as red as hers and by that much he'd been whittled down, made smaller in his own eyes; made—if the law ever got around to looking into it—an accessory to murder.

All have turned aside, together they have gone wrong. Brett remembered that passage from Scripture. *None is righteous, no, not one.* He guessed that pretty well summed it up.

He started filling in the hole.

Stoker wouldn't be sleeping too well hereafter, either. He'd got his head full of Lola and the increasing uncertainty of his prospects—caught as he was between two loyalties—would be giving him hell. The man needed his wages and, too old to catch on at anything else even if anything had here been available, the security of the job he already had. Which—come right down to it—was a chancey proposition under the best of conditions and was now further aggravated by his own divided allegiance, his need to remain in Jo's good graces tugging and twisting where the hair was short and every plaguing thought he had about Lola dragging him inexorably nearer the thundering sands of Jo's tumultuous wrath.

The kid's scowling face churned up into Brett's thoughts and the saturnine arrogant shape of Bill Tice was a black silhouette behind a cocked pistol. Either one of these would kill Brett the first good chance they had and they weren't like to waste much time being finicky. They'd be back here, both of them, swollen with hate.

Brett might block or hold away the kid. A few words to the marshal. . . . It would enrage Syd Stoker beyond any prod Brett might otherwise devise to learn what the kid had had in mind that day with Lola—that Red had actually put his hands on her. Brett was sorely tempted for it would cut this deal in half, freeing him to devote full time to Tice and Flagler.

He didn't know why he couldn't bring himself to do it. Playing them off against each other was the only sensible chance he had. The girl was mixed up with his reluctance—he wouldn't let himself look closer but it was there, inside him, steadily gnawing, jeering, compelling him toward disaster just as surely as its barbs were sunk in Stoker and, more wickedly, in the kid.

Lola. There was no calculated evil in her. It was simply her dark fortune to have a greater than ordinary capacity for passion while being denied by her location and peculiar circumstances the relief of conventional outlets. She was a woman rich with talent, crammed to bursting with impetuous needs she could not understand, trapped by her ignorance—completely alone.

Though he didn't put these things into those precise terms, Brett felt them and was shaken by them. Sensing the hurricane bottled so fiercely inside her, the torture and conflict, he knew only that she was fighting the deepest wellsprings of her being, afraid of herself, ashamed to acknowledge these desires and wild hungers, believing them to be abnormal, cheap, degrading.

He leveled off the grave, tramping the dirt down somberly, scattering what was left across the indentations of his tracks, telling himself he had to get out of here, knowing he would not go.

He was stuck with this now. The wolves were showing their fangs and every man's hand was against him. When he needed most to win he had nothing to hit back with. *Face it! Quit being a chump and get wise to yourself!*

Brett, glowering, clenched his fists. He could no longer hide behind a jerry-built wall of shifting words. He had to face the truth about Lola, admit he was seeing this through—had been here all along and come out in the first place—only because no other woman had ever got under his skin so deep. *Say it!*

"All right—I love her!" he snarled, and knew that at last he had told the whole truth.

20

BRETT tossed the shovel aside and struck off across the yard. He came onto the groaning planks of the porch and with an extreme reluctance moved into the house.

He'd no intention of letting Lola know. He was too miserably aware of his own unworthiness, of the curse of violence that would never let him go. He couldn't afford to think beyond this. He was nothing—less than nothing, his only reason for staying being the chance of doing whatever he might, knowing there could be no sequel to what he felt for this strange girl.

He found her standing before a window, slender—almost wraithlike in that uncertain light. She heard and brought herself around, facing him still-eyed, bracing herself in a way that hit him harder than tears ever could have.

The compulsion to take her into his arms almost overpowered him. It needed every ounce of control he had to stand so near and keep his hands off her; it brought the kid into his head and left him white-faced and shaken, bitterly conscious of his weakness, almost hating himself for the things that churned through him.

He said gruffly, "I've buried him," and the silence closed in again, an increasing awareness sharpening his hungers, the needs of the flesh rising up like sap in him. With an almost audible groan his eyes twisted away from her. He used what words he could lay hand to, trying to shove this thing away from them. "I'll put up the stove." He sounded like a fool, but he had to get out of there. "See if you can find somethin' to eat in this mess."

He whirled away, plunging into the kitchen, stumbling over

106

wrecked furniture, boots grating harshly on the shards of smashed dishes. He righted the stove that had been tipped over—a wood-burning range that at the time had been fortunately empty—found a rock to replace a leg that was missing, got the pipe back into its hole in the wall, coughing in the pall of black soot that shook out of it. He could hear Lola moving around and fiercely reduced a broken chair to sticks, stuffing them into the stove, never feeling the splinters that broke off in his hands. He got coal oil off the back stoop and built a fire up, shoved the lids back in place and took the can out.

Coming around to the front he got the Winchester Trone had loaned him and hunkered down with his back to the porch edge beside the rifle Stoker had left there, pulling Trone's pistol out of his shirt, checking the loads and anchoring the weapon in the waistband of his pants. He got out his pipe and put it away again, squatting there, blank-eyed, thinking about Flagler. He was still at it when Lola called.

He went in, lugging both rifles. He left them against the wall where they'd be handy and took the bent fork Lola handed him. They ate from the skillet, doggedly, not talking, each of them uncomfortably aware of the other and of the tension that was filling this room beyond bearing.

Brett went out when the food was gone and fetched a bucket of water, putting it down near what was left of the sink, not trusting his eyes, knowing she was watching him. Their nearness and the danger made him unconscionably awkward.

The house was suddenly too small; both of them knew it. Sweat came out on the backs of Brett's hands and he would have liked right then to have had Tice within reach. "I better pack out some of this stuff," he growled, glaring at it. There was hardly a stick of whole furniture left.

When he came back she was standing in the middle of the room.

He cut around her, heading for a ripped-apart section of the horsehair sofa someone of Tice's bunch had dragged out of the sitting room.

"Brett, we can't run away from this thing forever."

It stopped him cold. He couldn't breathe. He couldn't think. The thickening shadows mocked and taunted him. He knew she was waiting for him to face her, make some answer, and there were no words in him—none he dared speak.

His eyes took hold of the gouged wall fiercely yet he was acutely conscious of the way her hands came uncertainly out, of the feelings that turned her so blindly away, of the sound of her footsteps dropping like stones into the silence. Brett half turned, watching her, dark of face; and suddenly a mighty fear was in him. He broke out of his tracks and she whipped around with a catch of breath, head high, and came back, stopping directly in front of him.

Huskily, unknowingly, Brett Fasken swore.

His knees started shaking. A groan came out of him.

Both her hands came out and up to catch hold of him. He felt her fingers tight on his shoulders; and she was silent, head tilted, searching his face. He said hoarsely, marveling, "You're not afraid any more."

"I don't know. It's just. . . ." He could scarcely hear her. She was trembling again. In this dark he strained to read her expression, knowing the folly—unable to help himself.

He took hold of her elbows, clutching them painfully. He caught the gleam of her teeth. She cried fiercely, "I've found *you!* Nothing else matters!"

He broke, pulling her to him, and she clung, softly crying, with her face against his shirt, his own face buried in her hair.

21

BRETT spent a frustrating night at the barn, twisting, muttering, miserably staring into the smothering shadows, rebellious, hopeless, desperate by turn, unable to get his mind off what had happened—off what he knew in his bones was practically bound to happen. How in Christ's name could he have been so damned stupid! To comfort her, sure—any man could understand that, but coming right out with it, letting her see in her need how it was with him, letting her believe when he knew all the time. . . . He felt, by God, like taking a gun—

Opening up a whole new world to her!

Better had she never known than taste the ecstasy they had shared—that wild sweet bliss, the trembling joy, the blinding light that never again—

Brett cursed. It hadn't been his intention. It was just that, for a while, things had sort of got away from him and he had filled her head with a lot of damn foolishness. She figured they were at the beginning of something; Brett, despising himself, knew better.

Every alien sound brought him up, gun in hand—the creak and snap of settling timbers, rush of wind across the roof, wood striking wood, the clack of branches. Wasn't likely Tice would be back this quick, but there was Flagler and Red and Syd Stoker—maybe even Bud Lahr and the two-bitters Lahr spoke for. Any of these might show, and one well placed slug. . . .

Through sheer nervous exhaustion Brett finally slept, but it did him no good. He was up at first gray crack of dawn, red-eyed, faced with the enormity of his folly. To have given her hope that held no chance of fulfillment was unforgivable—cruel beyond anything Red had done. She had known every instant where she was with Red. Brett—God help him—had sowed the seeds of heartbreak through all of her tomorrows.

He went out and shoved his head in the trough, swashing his dripping hair back irascibly, glaring at the strengthening pink and cerise behind the humped hills rising out of the east. The heavy clouds above this were no blacker than his thoughts.

How could he tell her? *Look, Miss. That didn't figure. We just got carried away*. It was what a man ought to do.

He got a rag and cleaned his weapons, got some oats for Roanie who, whickering softly, shook his flax-maned head at Brett. Brett caught up another horse, getting a measure of grain for him too. A thread of smoke curled above the kitchen stovepipe. Brett went over still carrying the rifles.

Lola, blushing prettily, grabbed up a bowl and began beating hell out of something inside it. She had on a clean gingham dress and wore a scarlet ribbon in her hair. She was diffident, painfully conscious of herself and indescribably attractive. The wonder and the beauty of their relation had transformed her. "Think it's going to rain?"

Brett rubbed his jaws. He was not moved to wonder, too sunk in the morass of his own dark problems. She said, stirring vigorously, moving back to the stove, "I put Vic's razor over there on the window ledge. You've got perhaps three minutes."

Brett took the blade and went out to the trough. He was tempted to get on old Roanie and leave. Time he got himself scraped he'd made up his mind to one thing: This was no place for Lola. He rinsed off Vic's razor, wiping it dry on his shirt as he tramped back.

She was in the window hole, staring inscrutably off toward the south, turning when she heard his step. It gave him a twist the way her eyes lighted up. Her smile even further disquieted him. Temper made him want to lash out and smash something, and he understood better what had prompted Tice to wreck this place. Lola handed him the good fork, taking the bent one for herself— too happy, it seemed like, to let his before-breakfast scowls damp her outlook.

She had running-off of the mouth for sure, chattering away all the while Brett was eating. Though he managed an occasional grunt he gave little attention to the gist of her remarks; he was lost in thought. Tice, now committed, would strike again. This time he'd come with enough help to get the job done, then hit those other small-spread outfits and move in on Currycomb. Speed was essential; it was these ruthless tactics of surprise and shock which had built Hobbled O into the big spread it was. Success breeds success and, Brett thought grimly, carries the seeds of its own destruction.

When they were done he said, "We're going to Currycomb. Put on somethin' you can ride in. I'll saddle up."

In the stable he found an old banged-up canteen, the screw cap of it gone. He got it down off its peg and broke the peg off for a stopper, looping the carry-rope over a shoulder. Lola was ready when he returned with the horses. "Flagler won't help us."

"He's in this," Brett shrugged, "whether he likes it or not and he can't stand by himself. You got any loads for these rifles?"

He saw her concern. She said, more worried: "You can't buck this whole country."

Brett looked away from her and squinted at the sky. The sun was up but it was like it was coming through a stretch of old sacking. Everything looked queerly lemony. The air felt like it had been mixed with glue. "Get them shells if you got any an' let's get started."

She turned back inside and Brett, leaving their mounts on dropped reins, cut around to the rear of Trone's wrecked house, slipping the canteen's rope off his shoulder. He found what he was looking for right where he'd left it.

He was back with the horses when Lola came out with half a

box of mixed cartridges which he sorted, stowing the usable ones where they'd be handy. He affixed the canteen to the horn of his saddle and found her prolonged attention disturbing.

"Brett—what will we do?"

"See Flagler."

"I mean about—us." There was tension in her look, a mounting fright at the back of her stare. "You'll be all alone—" Her voice began to climb. "You'll be left like my brother!"

Brett laughed shortly.

"But this place isn't worth it!" she cried rebelliously. "I—I couldn't bear—"

Brett shut his ears and kicked the roan into motion.

CURRYCOMB had the scraped-bare look of an armed encampment. Flagler apparently had sized things up about the same as Brett and was not minded to be caught napping. A hundred yards from headquarters a bleach-eyed puncher stepped out of the hackberries cuddling a rifle and, looking them over, waved them on without remark. As they went past he loosed two shots overhead before ducking back in the brush. Brett said, "How much of a crew has Flagler got?"

"About a dozen, I think."

"Any women around?"

"Probably one in every closet and two or three under each bed."

Brett stared at her, shocked. He said after a moment, "You don't like him much, do you?"

"What cause has he given me?" She looked up at Brett. "He won't help—I should think you could see that. How do you know what Tice hasn't promised? Every move Flagler makes is weighed first for a profit." She shook her head irritably. "You're wasting your time."

However this went, Brett had hoped to leave her here, at least until he could think of something better. Now he wasn't so sure. A chill was settling deep into his bones and the old harrowing, frustrating blackness was chewing away the last thin hope he'd been clinging to.

Flagler's buildings, low squat boxes of unplastered adobe, showed narrow slots for windows and heavy plank shutters that could be yanked shut with drawstrings. Brett remembered this place, recalling that Flagler—when Fasken senior was still around—had displayed a considerable interest in Jo.

The man had toughened up a lot since then.

Lola kneed her mount alongside as Brett walked the roan toward Currycomb's owner, framed in an open ranch house door. No discernible expression was on the cattleman's fish-narrow face. His thumbs were hooked in his cartridge belt. There was the gleam of blued steel in the cracks of his eyes.

Brett picked out a man with a gun in the shadow of the stable arch, another silently crouched behind an open bunkhouse window. There were probably others, although with cattle to watch a crew of a dozen might be spread pretty thin. He kept his attention on Flagler. Flagler was staring at the girl.

"That's far enough," he called when they were ten feet short of the porch.

Brett folded both hands across the horn of his saddle. "Wouldn't want you to be gettin' any wrong ideas."

"Sooner you're out of here the better I'll like it."

"Conscience hurtin'?"

Flagler said, "Speak your piece an' get whackin'."

"Thought mebbe you might of had a change of heart after that ride you took yesterday with Tice. Even went so far as to figure you might be wantin' to hole up with us."

Flagler's veins bulged a little. Livid patches broke out along the sides of his jaws and Brett, watching him, said before the man could kill all chance of further talk, "Keepin' what a feller's got is—"

"Don't you worry about that!"

"You're worryin' enough for both of us. Reckon you been thinkin' how you'll look laid out in a box or mebbe left someplace for the birds an' coyotes." Brett gave him a hard stare. "Can't say as I blame you. But you don't have to sit around waitin' for Tice—"

"Now ain't that the truth! I could put a slug through you an'—"

Lola cried, "Don't you feel anything at all about my brother?"

Flagler's face got red. He took a half step back. "Now look here—you got no call to— Wasn't *me* killed Vic!"

"You might just as well have. You were there. You didn't stop them."

Flagler looked as though his face had been too near to a fire and, in an infuriated voice that cracked in frightened outrage, shouted: "You don't know what you're talkin' about!" A muscle jerked high up in one cheek and the fingers of his hands were closing and opening like a buzzard's talons. A crafty look crossed his face. "Who says I was there—this trouble-huntin' drifter?"

Lola astonished both men by conjuring from somewhere a nickel-plated pistol. Flagler let out a bleat and Brett made a grab for her wrist and by great luck got hold of it. The fierceness of her struggles almost brought him out of the saddle before he twisted the weapon away from her.

Both horses were dancing, half minded to pitch. Men were hollering. In the midst of this uproar Flagler commenced to yell like a looney: "*Cut 'im down—cut 'im down!*"

One look at the rancher told Brett he wasn't fooling. Except for Lola's horse getting his head down, humping into a series of half-hearted jumps between Brett and the pair cached in bunkhouse and stable, he reckoned they'd have done it. As it was, the girl's position gave him a chance to spin the roan. But Lola wasn't in Flagler's way and now he had his gun up. It was plain by the way he was throwing down on them, he didn't care which he hit; and it came over Brett the man was trying to buy his way with them into Tice's good graces.

Yanking the girl's animal around by the check strap Brett carried him along until both horses were stretching; then, turning loose, he cut the gray with his rein ends. "Ride!" he shouted.

Flagler's gun was pounding and lead was ripping and chuffing, the sound vicious as hornets. All about the yard other weapons were throwing out bursts of black powder as the squealing horses plunged into the hackberry jungle. Brett and Lola—bent as low as the horns of their saddles permitted—each held an arm folded ahead of and over them to fend off the worst of the slashing branches.

Brett was white with outrage, shaking with fury, when the brush got thick enough to stop slugs behind them, walling them off from that murderous barrage. "Keep goin'!" he growled when it seemed like Lola might be minded to do otherwise. "Don't stop, for Christ's sake!"

They'd be saddling back there. Flagler couldn't quit now and nothing but God's own mercy, Brett thought, was like to get Lola out of this. Every moment she remained in his company was shortening her chances by just that much. They might kill her anyway if they got hold of her out here, but there was no room for doubt should they catch her with Brett.

He ran the horses ten minutes, hating to, scared not to. When they came out of the brush in a vista of ridges he knew they would have to keep away from Trone's headquarters. It was the first place Currycomb, if their trail were lost, would make for. Lola's best bet, like Stoker had told her, was town. Brett figured it a waste of breath to suggest this. Nothing he might say was like to shake her loose—she knew what Tice's bunch would do if they caught him.

He hauled the roan to a walk. Both horses were blowing. He

had no way of knowing how far back Flagler was. He could feel Lola watching but couldn't bring himself to look at her, knowing here was some of the hell he'd bought last night.

He was soaked with sweat; the horses' coats were dark with it. The air was sticky, like Yuma in August. "Sun's gone," Lola said, surprised. Looking up, Brett could find nothing but clouds, so low they looked to be draping the hills, trapping the heat like the spread of a blanket, gray and forlorn as old wool past the shearing. Brett's mind could find no escape. There was no safe place they could make for, no hole that he could find through which Lola might be pushed to safety without he took her to town; and he was considering this, knowing what the marshal would do if he saw Brett, when the girl cried his name.

She was gray and rigid. "Off there!"

Brett's sweat-stung eyes whipped to where she was pointing. The whole world felt like it was dropping from under him. Topping out across a ridge not half a mile away was a file of mounted men, Tice at the front of them—and back of Brett somewhere was Flagler and Currycomb.

The west and north were closed up solid. East was the wasted land beyond Trone's, the commonwealth of small spreads, none of whom would lift a hand for a Fasken. South was the town, maybe thirty miles away. Together they were whipped but the girl, if he could pull off the riders, might make it.

22

TICE of course had seen them and was coming up fast, now showing, now lost in the broken ground between. Though nearly noon it was dark as eight—darker, really—and there was a lot of dust. "I'll catch you later—make for town!" Brett yelled, and brought his reins down across Lola's horse.

The gray bolted, beyond her power to control or turn, and Brett put spurs to the blowing roan, whirling him back into the draw they'd come out of, crowding him north in the direction of Currycomb. Tice, at least, didn't want the girl; he was champing to fetch Brett into his sights and, for right now, had mind for nothing else.

Brett was still mulling around an idea he'd got during breakfast, his reason for bringing this canteen along. If he could just elude Tice long enough to break through—if he could keep them from driving him into Flagler's guns. . . .

That was asking a lot but there was a bend back here someplace. He kept pushing the roan, trying to gain cover before Tice could knock him out of the saddle. That Hobbled O bunch was sure riding their stirrups; he could hear the faint cork-stopper popping of their rifles. *Where the hell was that bend?*

Now they were pounding into the draw, its slopes magnifying their racket. Slugs began kicking up spurts of sand. The roan humped under Brett, pulling his rump in, squealing and breaking pace. The horse was hit but Brett kept him running, cursing bitterly. He could see the bend through the tatters of dust flung ahead by the wind. *Keep goin'—keep goin'.*

Queer what pictures the mind dredged up. Brett thought of the mistakes he'd come back here to right—*a goddam Quixote!* The meek might inherit like the Good Book said, but not around here. You didn't stop a Bill Tice by turning the other cheek.

Brett knew without looking back how little time he had. They'd keep right on coming till they ran him into the ground or dropped him with a lucky shot. They had all the advantage of fresher horses, thorough knowledge of the country and the weight of numbers. But the roan was running steadily again, body stretched, legs flogging. There was just a bare chance. . . . All depended, Brett thought, on whether or not Currycomb had got out of the hackberries—this wind was blowing the racket right at them.

And here was the bend. Brett went into the turn, hauling the roan's head up, hearing the shouts of Tice's outfit back of him. His glance flashed ahead, but he saw no sign of Flagler. He slammed the horse at the near bank and drove him up it through the yellowing fronds of heat-parched salt cedar. The bank was sloped but steep, scarcely ten foot here, yet Brett wondered if they were ever going to make it. Stones and gravel noisily slipped under the hoofs of the straining roan and Brett flung himself out of the saddle, climbing through the growth of breaking branches and hauling the stumbling horse along after him. Sweat poured off his flushed face and the shouting racket of Tice's riders echoed around him in the wind until it almost seemed they were right on his shirttail.

They weren't. They hadn't yet rounded the bend, though they were almighty close as he came out on flat ground. As he dragged the horse up out of the brush he saw the bloody streak of scuffed-up hide where the Hobbled O slug had creased the animal's hip. Brett was as short of breath as the horse; he stood there beat, half crouched, eyes bulging, aware of the sudden throbbing silence below them.

"By God," Tice said flatly, "he must of—"

"There! Ain't that Flagler's bunch comin' out of. . . ."

Brett didn't wait to hear any more. With thumping heart he eased away from the rim, drawing Roanie after him. What sound they made was whipped away by the wind, by the surprise and spattering onslaught of the first fat drops of rain.

Rain!

Brett twisted a narrowing glance overhead, baring his face to it, feeling it pelting him, seeing the dark boil of black sky above. By God, if that wasn't the way of things! Drive these poor bastards right onto their knees then soak the damn country to push up grass Jo didn't need and couldn't no way use without she grabbed up their cattle along with everything else!

He got back in the saddle, knowing he dared not delay any longer. He had this chance and that was all. The rain—if it didn't plumb quit on him—would probably wash out his tracks if he could gain enough ground. He'd have to pile up a lead and this was all open country for the next couple miles if he went the way he'd figured to go—and there was no other way he *could* go now. No other direction was open to him. It had to be west-southwest. Somewhere off there, out of sight, was Hobbled O.

They were bound to see him. No getting around it. He had left plain sign gouging into that bank, and some of them were swarming up it right now, snap of brush and sliding shale reaching him even through the wild gust of wind.

NOT all of Jo's crew, when Tice left to hunt Brett, had gone with the range boss as he set off for Currycomb. Jo, Tice and the kid had gone over this carefully. Because Flagler was still the wild card in this deal they'd decided to keep part of the crew with the cattle, just in case. It was Tice's opinion Flagler hadn't the guts to come out openly against them, but he agreed with Jo that Brett would probably try to talk him around to it; and there was always the chance—like the kid suggested—that Flagler, if the man were desperate enough, might try some kind of undercover shenanigan. Tice had his own ideas of how to deal with Flagler. All three of them, Jo included, saw eye to eye on the subject of Brett. Brett had to go. "You can't reason with him," Jo said, convinced in her own mind he'd come back to shoulder into this. "The only thing Brett'll understand is a bullet."

And Red was aching to give it to him.

Tice shared the feeling. But Tice wasn't interested at all in Trone's sister. When they sighted the pair several miles short of Currycomb and saw Brett stampede the girl's horse toward town, all Tice cared about was coming up with Brett—getting near enough anyhow to make sure Brett would never bother nobody else.

The whole push seemed suddenly to be taken with this craziness. Shouting, yelling, they went gun-waving after Brett.

Like a pack of damn fools riding after a hound, the kid thought, pulling up. Sitting there with his lip curled he watched Hobbled O larrup through the curtains of dust.

This couldn't have suited Red better if he had planned it. Now things were starting to come his way! Opportunity was banging the door with both fists—he could settle with Jo or he could go after Trone's sister.

Inclination was tugging him mightily in both directions. This was his chance to lay the law down to Jo. She was at the ranch with no one around but that stove-up cook; he could drive her to town right now, get the knot tied, and clinch his hold on Hobbled O, by God, so no one could shake him loose of it!

His head told him to do it while Tice and her brother had their hands full someplace else. But all his instincts kept pushing in the other direction. He could handle Jo any time; Tice would take care of Brett and things could happen to Tice like his gun going off while he was fixing to clean it. But never again might he have as good a chance to slap his brand on that luscious Lola.

Just the thought set his veins afire, and he spun his horse with a wet-lipped grin. There would be no Brett to break it up this time.

SYD Stoker, after he got back to town, spent an even worse night than Brett had, going over and over what he'd said and done—bothered even more by the things he might have done and hadn't.

He was a man past his prime—as a gun handler anyway—long past the time when security was just another word to be laughed at. Because he'd been afraid to turn loose of his job he had temporized, compromised with what he had figured to be his plain-out duty, trying to straddle as he'd been doing for the past couple years a fence that was just about to come apart under him.

This country was going to blow hell west and crooked and Stoker knew a gnawing shame for the hands-off stand he'd been attempting to justify. He kept remembering Lola's look when she had refused to return to town with him, and his wretchedness was something he could no longer live with. He had never imagined the girl was in love with him and had known his own feelings had no chance of a future, but he might with more gumption have kept her respect.

He heard the first rooster crow and came irascibly out of his lumpy bunk, pulling on his boots, running a hand through his hair, peering at his reflection in the piece of cracked mirror. Damn near gray as Jo Fasken!

There'd been a time when this country had looked up to him. Maybe it wasn't too late yet. Brett's face came before him and he remembered Brett saying he'd come back to start over. Still thinking about this Stoker got his razor and scowlingly stropped it.

What Jo was doing to this country wasn't right and no amount of talk would make it right. Nobody knew any better than Syd what was like to happen if he got in her way. The loss of his badge was the least of his problems and, suddenly, those problems were no longer important.

He shaved carefully and washed and, frowning, dragged a brush through his hair. He still had the badge; until they took it away he was all the law there was in this country.

He went back into the office, rummaged in his desk and got a short-barreled pistol, dropping it into his pocket. It was too hot for a coat but he kept it on anyway, even though he wore no tie at his throat. He left his belt gun where it was on a nail, not bothering with spare cartridges. The place to start, he guessed, was Schultz, or with what had happened to Trone at Scab 8.

He went over to the livery and grained his horse, shook hay into the rack and went across to the restaurant. It was full day now, an uncommonly gray one. By the look of those clouds it could be shaping up for a gully-washer. He took a stool at the counter and presently was eating. A couple of merchants came in though it was still pretty early. Both men ignored him. Stoker was used to this. "Looks like rain," the hasher said. The shorter man snorted. Buck Benton—he owned the saddle shop—said, "If it does there's goin' to be a lot of drowned frogs."

Stoker signaled for another cup of coffee and, when he'd drunk it empty, paid and walked back over to the livery. He waited around while his horse finished the hay, got him a drink in a bucket and put the saddle on him. He was cinching up when the hostler looked in at him. "Goin' someplace?"

"I'd go fishin'," Stoker said, "if I knew where there was any."

He got aboard and rode out and stepped down in front of the office. He stepped inside and reappeared carrying a Sharps rifle chambered for the .45-120-550—a he-man deal in anybody's language. He got into the saddle still holding this formidable weapon and was about to knee his commands to the horse when the boy who swamped for the Coffin Bar—this was the place that advertised women—put his head out the door, eyes big as pullet eggs.

"Gosh, Mister Stoker! You're loaded fer bear ain'cha?"

Stoker looked a little sheepish.

"You goin' after them highbinders out to Hobbled O?"

Stoker fiddled with his reins. "Just figurin' to sight this gun in is all, Bob. How're your folks makin' it?"

"Aw, we're still eatin'." The boy said indignantly, "Pap, he says you wouldn't git off your ass—jest wait'll I tell 'em! You're not scairt of *nothin'* are you? Gee," he said, squirming, scuffing bare feet, "you couldn't find no use fer a depity could you?"

Stoker couldn't think what to say hardly. He cleared his throat. "Tell you what," he growled finally, "I'll keep you in mind. I don't look for no trouble but if it turns out I'm wrong we'll see if we can't sort of figure out somethin'."

23

JO Fasken was unaccountably restless—even queerly uneasy wandering through the big house and knowing it was empty, understanding this day might well decide the outcome of all she'd set her hand to. The dark and echoing rooms depressed her, harboring ghosts she had thought to have laid behind the carefully erected masonry of her mind.

She made an impatient effort to shrug off this mood, ascribing it to the sunless light, and glared defiantly at lowering clouds which shut out the sky—almost as though to remind her there were things in this world not even she could control. She didn't want rain—her cows had no need of it; she didn't want the hope of it buoying up those greasy-sackers hanging on in frustrating stubbornness to ground that, by all the work she'd put into this, should by rights be an extension of Hobbled O.

Why couldn't they read their inevitable end in the dust that lifted in ragged banners wherever a wind came across powdered soil? There were signs—any number; the stubborn fools should have gone, making way for the empire she was putting together, not stupidly staying without credit or hope.

She didn't want their damned blood on her hands. Violence sickened her. It was like a curse put on her, yet she had no intention of letting Brett or anyone else keep her from this. She would do what she had to.

The most of her disquiet, she bitterly imagined, was traceable to Brett and the orders she had given this morning concerning him. Well, he'd known what he could look for, sneaking back after he'd said he would stay out of this country. She'd not tolerate interference.

Memory of Clint wildly throbbed in her head as it always did when she got Brett on her mind. Just to think of Brett was like waving a red rag at her fury. All those wretched empty nights she had known, the barren misery, the frustrations; she sometimes felt she was nothing but a bundle of jangling nerves—and all because of Brett. Damn him! No one but Clint had ever truly understood her.

Let Brett take his chances! She'd told him in no uncertain terms on the night Clint died to get out and stay out of everything concerning her, to never come back—and he'd defied her —that's what it amounted to. He'd threatened Red.

Tice would take care of him. Tice wasn't afraid of blood; sometimes she thought Tice actually gloried in it, proud of the way men cringed away from him. Mora, too, with his leaping guns and crazy half-breed eyes. And there was the kid himself—the whole crew she could call on!

Against these men Brett was nothing. He would know that.

Feeling vaguely better she went and got herself some milk from the crock in the well-house just beyond the kitchen stoop. Carrying the glass, sipping from it, tonguing her lips like a satisfied cat, she strolled back through the mirrorless rooms to stand again by the office window, not seeing the dusty hoof-chopped yard but looking through it, beyond it, seeing the dimensions of Hobbled O with all these other spreads added to it.

A sense of well-being began to work its way through her, lifting that intolerable burden of futility, pushing back the encroaching fog of unacknowledged dread, timbering her confidence with remembered victories and bolstering it with the power of her connections, the alliances she had made with people who counted.

No man could tear these from her!

Let Brett try, her mind scoffed. Just let him! She laughed at the picture of anyone attempting to unite that gutless bunch of small owners. Even Flagler would know better than to beat his head against such crass stupidity. A glance at the banjo clock put the time at ten forty-five. Scattered drops of rain were just commencing to fall, pushing up little boils of dust where they hit. She finished the milk and set the glass aside.

She went across to the desk, a battered roll-top affair that had been her father's. Because the room seemed so dark she put a match to the wick of the lamp standing on it. A sudden need of light to push away the black doubts drove her around to the bracketed pair on the wall and the Argand roundwick lamp on the marble-topped table that gave out so much brilliance—as much as ten or twelve candlepower—a lot of people wouldn't have them for fear of ruining their eyes.

The room, filled with light, sounded like the inside of a drum as the rain now came down in sheets outside, whipping against the walls like flung gravel. She had never seen it rain so hard. Lightning came in jagged streaks and thunder dogged her from room to room, rolling its monster reverberations through the house like the boom of rocks being dropped through a chute.

Not until she had the place closed tight and was sweating freely did she realize the absurdity of trapping all this heat. She went around reopening the windows on the east, discovering with vexation the widening pools coming in under the doors. She hunted rags then to stop it and other rags to sop it up. And still the thunder crashed. The knickknacks rattled in their corner whatnots and something fell off a wall somewhere, and when she put her face against the streaming glass to peer nervously in the direction of the cookshack all the yard in between was a lake of gray water.

A cooped-up feeling began to come over her, a foreboding she was in no mood to cope with; she ran back to the lighted office and got her father's gun from a drawer of the desk and, feeling too exposed there, drew the shades to the sills in a fluster of movement.

This was ridiculous! Her mind tried to assert itself, to banish the crazy things in her head, the edginess that had hold of her.

The flapping of the shades over the open east windows kept sawing at her nerves. With a frantic cry she went and snapped them up and stood there staring at the wind-driven rain, the miniature torrents noisily pouring off the eaves. All the washes would be up, travel would practically be at a standstill if this kept on. It might be hours. . . . She thought of Tice and the crew, worried only that this might delay the fruition of her plans, hardly thinking of the men as such, more bothered about what Flagler might try if he was able to get around them.

Next time she thought to look at the clock it was five till twelve and the rain was still coming down. But things were noticeably lighter, as though the worst of the storm were moving away. She could see half across the yard when she looked—there must be all of a foot of water out there at the very least. The cookshack and bunkhouse were just gray blobs through the still falling slant of it, and she couldn't see the corrals at all.

She felt a twinge of compunction as she thought of Brett being hounded—maybe wounded, somewhere out in that wet. But she hardened her heart. He owned no call on her after all he had done, after what he had said to her right in this room. He deserved whatever happened. In sudden fury she hoped he was dead.

The rain settled into a steady drizzle. The poles of the corral emerged from the downpour and she saw the cook stick his head from the door about the time she got through pulling up the rest of the shades. She felt suddenly ravenous and debated wading over on the chance of taking pot luck with him, finally deciding to munch on what she could find. She was headed for the kitchen when the sounds jerked her up.

Staring through the office window across the yard she saw the sodden shape of the dripping horseman and stiffly froze, watching intently, eyes wide in the sudden pallor of her face. It couldn't be—yet it was! No one else sat a horse in quite that way. It was Brett! *Where was Red? Where was Mora? Where was Tice and the crew!*

If they were after him Brett wasn't letting it bother him. She realized with a quavery knot in her stomach he must have lost them in the storm.

He came on through the pools, the slippery splash and squish of mud, without hurry, steadily nearing, dogmatic in this as in everything he did. Nothing, she thought bitterly, ever flustered Brett! Nothing ever stopped him when he set those bulldog jaws.

She felt close to panic. Why was he coming here? What did he think that would get him? Was he fool enough to imagine she would. . . . No—not Brett. He must still be determined to stop her. He was coming here to. . . .

Almost with a sense of shock she discovered she still had her father's gun in her hand.

24

IT was the half-breed, Mora, who was fighting his horse up the bank after Brett. All the rest of Tice's crew pulled up back of the ramrod, watching Flagler's outfit straggle out of the hack-berries. The Currycomb boss, red-faced and blasphemous, threw up a hand at the clot of Hobbled O riders. Wind tore his words away but none of them stood in any doubt of his meaning. He still hoped to mediate—not for Brett but for his own place, his ranch and his range.

Tice, as solid in the saddle as though a part of the big horse under him, sat with his face like a gout of thrown clay. You might read whatever you were minded to into it, anything or nothing; his thoughts were too well hidden to show and Flagler, coming up, put on a bluff look, persuading himself he had nothing to worry about until Tice got rid of the small outfits bordering them. Tice would be glad of his help up to then.

If Tice was he didn't show it.

Flagler licked his lips. "Went up that bank, didn't he? We damn near had him nailed at the ranch for you—would of done it, too, if the girl had kep' out of it."

Rain was beginning to fall. He saw the wet marks of it on Tice's blocky chin—the black shine of Tice's stare. A dryness got into Flagler's throat and all the quieted doubts rose up again to gnaw at him. It was the cold, flat, uncompromising tone of the man's clipped words that dragged Flagler out of his tangled think-ing. "Eh?" He jerked up his head like the jump of a rabbit.

"I said what was he doin' there?" All the power of Hobbled O bristled out of Tice like knife blades.

"To tell you the truth," Flagler spoke too loud out of his frightened confusion, "he come over to see 'f he couldn't talk me into backin' 'em. . . ."

His breath wizzled out.

They were watching him, all those wind-ruddied, weather-darkened faces back of Tice. The rain came down harder and, except for this, it got quieter and quieter. He didn't want to look at Tice and was afraid to twist his eyes away. Why didn't the son of a bitch say something!

Flagler wanted to slip a quick look at his crew. If he'd been sure of them he never would have been in this predicament; he was afraid Tice knew this.

It was the poker-cheeked disinterest of Tice's look that really boogered him; he'd been a fool to come out of those hackberries.

"Expect you told him," Tice murmured idly, "that when the chips was down you'd be stringin' with Hobbled O."

"Yeah— Hell, yes!" Flagler's voice squeaked with eagerness. "That's exactly what I told him—"

"You made a mistake."

The mildness of Tice's tone, the smile lurking around the shining edges of his teeth, almost robbed the words of significance. Flagler was opening his mouth, minded to emphasize his virtue, when the full sense of them suddenly hit him.

Knowledge seeped through the damp blanch of his cheeks. He let go of his rifle. With his eyes like squeezed grapes he settled both shaking hands in plain sight on his saddle. He was that way, still staring, when the roar of Tice's gun knocked him out of it.

Smiling, watching the man's frozen crew, Tice replaced the spent shell with a cartridge from his belt. Rain made the only other sound in that stillness. Even the wind slunk away.

The burly range boss rummaged their faces. "Shorty, I can

use you—git over here. I'll take you too, Salazar, an' your wetback compadre in the big hat there. Rest of you jaspers," his cold stare pushed among them, "head out an' head fast. I see any of you again you'll wind up with the buzzards."

No one opened his mouth. The most of them picked up their reins and turned south. One or two headed back toward the ranch for their belongings. Tice let them go, not minded to push his luck too far; this could still get ugly if somebody got his back up.

The wind came again and Tice chopped a hand down. "All right, boys. Mora's huntin' Fasken. Let's see if we can find him."

WHEN at last the storm began to pull away, Lola hadn't the foggiest notion where she had got to. It seemed as though she'd been lost in this downpour forever—even her mind was going numb. Bone weary, prey to aches and uncertainty, she tried to recall how many times unexpectedly she'd been confronted with raging torrents of impassable water, forced off her path, battered and deafened in a streaming wind-hammered world of crashing thunder and lighting. She remembered one terrifying sequence of toppling trees, of branches crazily flying through the rain-beaten dark.

Brett had started her south, this was all she was sure of. She had tried to get back to him but when she had gotten the bolting horse under control the cloudburst had swallowed Brett, wiping out all horizons, reducing visibility to something under three horse lengths, fencing her in with slashing walls of lance-gray water. Confused, panicked, trying to put down her fears for Brett, she had attempted belatedly to do as he'd told her, thinking to use the wind for a guide.

But the wind had shifted—she'd known this finally, finding it first on one side, then on the other; some places it had appeared to come from all sides at once. How far she'd come since discovering it had tricked her she had no idea and no means for measuring. Shivering wretchedly she guessed she might have been going round in circles—lost people often did.

Gradually, now, the rain was subsiding, dwindling into a kind of chilled drizzle with the wind shrieking after the storm. Portions of the surrounding landscape, still sopping and puddled, began to take on recognizable shapes, but no part of it looked familiar.

Soaking, cold, and shivering uncontrollably, she tried to find shelter, but there simply wasn't any that she could see. This was a country of brush, head high, almost a brasada like the jungles of south Texas, only mostly this was greasewood with a scattering of thorny mesquite; the South Texas brush was chaparral, miles of it impenetrable. She tried to think whether she had heard of any region like this, but her mind was too weary to remember it if she had. She kept wretchedly going, determined to get out of it. The wet slapping of branches was indescribable torture. When higher country presently showed to the right she reined toward it.

But this was farther away than it looked. After more than an hour of slogging in this direction the brush gave way to a long saucerlike flat broken only by occasional waist-high clumps of pear cactus; the hills looked about as far away from her as ever. But at some time gone unnoticed the rain had quit. Discovering this she looked up. The sky was still hidden behind leaden clouds.

There was no one to see her, but an innate modesty turned her back into the brush where she got out of the saddle and peeled off her wet clothes right down to the skin. She couldn't help it— she simply had to. She wrung them out as best she could. Then, because her teeth were chattering and she could not hope to dry her clothes better, she put the still-damp things back on. Her horse looked about as miserable as she did. Her eyes, going past him, focused again on the hills and suddenly, astounded, she knew where she was. Those weren't hills, they were mountains—the

Galiuros, probably thirty miles off! She was east of Packer's Crossing, perhaps seven miles to the north of it!

RHODE Island Red, after losing the girl in the storm, rode crazily in skittering ever-widening circles trying to find her shape again through the gray veils of rain. He like to have run his mount into the ground before his fury would let him admit she'd got clear of him. For a while after that he just sat there, dripping and cursing.

Then, abruptly, he straightened, a grin slowly twisting his lips with new guile. Of course! That was it! He laughed hoarsely. She'd been making for town. All he had to do was get there, and wait, and pick her up when she came in.

Be just like falling off a log.

STOKER, the Packer's Crossing marshal, was still pointed north when the rain overtook him. He got into his fish, the yellow oilskin slicker (called so because of its trademark, a fish) much in vogue among cowmen and which most of the old-timers kept rolled behind their cantles. He hunched the rifle up under this covering, considering himself a fool to be out in this. But as he kept slogging along, his mind turned to Lola and all his thoughts became dreary as he recalled the shifts with which he'd covered past mistakes. He'd been a fool, all right, playing along with Hobbled O, letting Jo Fasken get a stranglehold on this country. Likely he was about to make himself a bigger one but at least by God he'd be his own fool now!

It was a good feeling—one he hadn't known in years. It sustained him through the next five miles, which were not easy on either him or the horse. Man was made for a saddle and he'd been too damn long away from his. Still he went on. He didn't try to figure out what he would say when he got there, but his mind, like a stereopticon kept showing him pictures that were pretty depressing.

Stoker didn't haul on the reins till he was halfway to Scab 8 headquarters, and it wasn't the visions he'd been having that stopped him then. He simply and suddenly knew there wouldn't be anybody there. Of course there wouldn't. Fasken had been too long in tune with trouble to stay propped up there on his hunkers waiting for Tice to make a colander out of him. Brett would know he had to have help, that there was no place he could get any short of Bud Lahr and the greasy-sackers Lahr did the talking for.

The marshal reined his horse east. It never occurred to him that Brett, long away, would seek out Flagler. Washes and gullies that hadn't known water in the past three years were now running bank to bank and forced him off his track a dozen times. It was nearing noon with rain still falling when Stoker pulled up, cursing, knowing just how big a damn fool he had been.

This was Saturday!

All the small-spread owners would be in town or trying to get there.

25

BRETT, pulled up by the gallery, did not at once swing down but, twisting around in the soggy squish of soaked clothes, slanted a look toward the cookshack, caught by the tang of wood smoke drifting out across this raw dampness. How well he remembered —how sharply the grip of half forgotten times dug into him. Hobbled O.

He dragged his nostalgic thoughts away from it and called up the things he had come here to do, trying to steel himself, trying to convince himself no man bucking Tice could afford the luxury of sentiment—knowing he could never go through with it. He'd come to burn Jo out, to crack that façade of contemptuous arrogance, to leave a mark that would show this whole range how to reach her—but the place was too much a part of him. The only really good days he'd ever known—

"Brett," Jo said, "get away from there!"

His eyes jerked back, finding her through the window in the brightness of the office, the battered desk that had been Brett's father's only partially concealing her. He saw the shelf of dusty novels that had given his dad so much quiet pleasure—Dickens, Irving, some of the newer American writers like Cooper; knowing the only books Jo found time for were the ledgers in which she computed ranch profits. The rain-wet glass distorted her features so that it was impossible to guess what purpose had hold of her, but something of what she felt he could sense in the wire-drawn stiffness of the way she stood glaring, never bending so much as one hand in his direction.

He had the canteen's rope twisted over his shoulder and, never thinking about this, got out of the saddle as Jo caught up a stamp iron and hurled it through the window. With the rain practically stopped this made racket enough to fetch the cook out of his shack, and lead from the man's rifle drove a black and vicious hole into a roof support scant inches from Brett's astonishedly jerked-around head.

"Hey!" Brett yelled, thinking the man didn't recognize him. "It's Brett Fasken, you—"

Again the rifle cracked. Brett felt the wind of that slug touch his cheek. Outraged, he ducked behind the snorting horse, yanking his Winchester. But he was wrong thinking the old man had gone loco—how wrong he found out when Jo, firing from the office, put a slug through his shirt. It was like someone had raked a knife across his ribs.

The whole look of Brett turned wicked. He dived under the horse's belly, levering a cartridge into place as he came up, firing almost at once. All he got was a click. Behind him the horse went down, thinly screaming and thrashing as the cook's gun blazed again. Catching the man in his sights, at the last instant lowering the muzzle a little, Brett squeezed trigger. The cartridge exploded. The cook spun and collapsed, letting go of the rifle.

Brett twisted aside, rolling in the muck of the yard as Jo tried again to get at him with the pistol. He could feel the thump of those shots all around him, shocking, confusing him, roweling his passions. He came up on one arm but couldn't bring himself to do more than glare at her. He snarled, "You taken leave of your senses?"

Out of the corner of his vision he glimpsed the cook crawling after the dropped rifle. A bullet from the office jerked the collar of Brett's mud-smeared shirt. Something snapped in him then. He broke the round-wick lamp with a slug to drive her to cover and reared up on both knees, eyes bright cracks in the wet pallor of his face. The cook had his rifle and was attempting to steady it across one knee. Brett killed him without compunction.

Lunging onto his feet in the squishy gumbo of the puddled yard, letting go of the Winchester, Brett dived onto the gallery, skidding on mud-caked boot heels, crashing into the wall, hanging there hard-breathing, heart pounding his ribs as he waited, teeth showing, for her to fire at him again. He was watching the broken window waiting for her to show when the sound of hoofs cutting over the yard pulled his head around. He saw the half-breed Mora, hair plastered over his hatless forehead, fling himself off the horse and come splashing forward with a gun in each hand.

Brett cursed himself for letting go of his Winchester. With the saddle gun he could have kept Mora back—without it he was a sitting duck for a man who had spent his whole life pistoleering. It came over Brett suddenly why Jo wasn't firing. She was reloading her weapon. In about three more jumps Mora would get into this. Brett saw his guns coming up, saw the man's wicked grin. Mora, that grin said, was going to enjoy this.

Slashing a hand at his belt Brett drove his left shoulder crashing into the door. There came a squeal of rending wood as the latch was ripped from the splintered casing. Brett, off balance, stumbled reeling into the lamp-lighted office, still pawing for the pistol—not finding it, dismally knowing he must have lost it in that roll.

No matter. He'd get Jo's.

He scrinched his eyes against that searing brightness and heard her yell at him. He had these few moments while he was out of Mora's reach. He saw Jo's wild eyes, saw the flame gout out of her leveled sixshooter—felt the whip of it, the twisting wrench at his shoulder. Something slapped his hip. He grabbed at her but she jumped back, hit the desk and careened off it screaming as the lamp toppled and broke.

The whole place seemed to explode in a monstrous *whuff!* Flame roared, enveloping them. Only then did Brett realize Jo's bullet, missing him, had torn through the canteen still slung from his shoulder. The coal oil he'd filled it with was spurting all over. He ducked, twisting out of the rope, just as Mora opened up through the window. Jo staggered back, falling into the wall with her jaws stretched wide in a scream that wouldn't come. Brett lunged over there thinking to carry her out but Mora never gave him the chance. Mora, grinning hugely, began firing both guns.

Brett could hear the slugs biting into things. His boots, plashed with oil, were beginning to burn—flame raced up the legs of his Levis. He caught up Jo's dropped gun as Mora's bullets struck around him. The fool was firing too fast, gripped by the lust of the madness inside him. Brett, wanting to get down below the level of the sill, knew better than to risk it in that inferno of blazing oil. But he had to get out—the heat was turning him crazy.

He broke for the door crouched low, flinging into a dive when he struck the planks of the gallery. He slipped on the edge, skidding off into gumbo, wallowing. A slug spun him half around. He lost his balance again, went down in the slop, managed to get a knee under him. He shoved himself out of it, finding Mora's frantic eyes. He took deliberate aim. Jo's gun bucked and roared. He watched the half-breed driven backward break at the middle —both hands clapped over his belly—and flop forward into the ooze.

26

THE Hobbled O crew, bunched back of Tice, sat sullenly astride their steaming horses watching the pall of flame-laced smoke trapped so darkly by lowering clouds above the ruined Fasken ranch headquarters. "Brett—God damn him!" snarled Tice, almost beside himself.

It was obvious to all that here had been no accident. Lightning had been known to do uncommonly queer things; it might have struck and burned one building, but it wouldn't have fired them all.

Tice, still swearing, roweled his horse into a run, the others following less precipitantly, glancing about them uneasily. When they came gingerly into the yard Tice was already bent over Mora. It seemed evident too that while they'd come a little late to intercept the breed's killer some of these buildings hadn't long been afire.

Tice straightened, twisting a long look at the collapsed office wing of the gutted house. If Jo was around and still alive why didn't she show?

A big-boned lanky rannihan with a shock of russet hair suddenly lifted a pointing hand. Turning, three or four of those nearest spotted the cook's huddled shape half submerged in the muck. A couple of them swore. One man closed a hand around the butt of his pistol.

Another, on the fringe, wheeled his mount out of the group. Tice's growl leaped after him: "Where you figger you're goin'?" Two others, about to pick up their reins, let them lay, visibly nervous.

The one spoken to said, "I'm by Gawd gettin' outa this!"

"I'll take care of that."

Maybe the man didn't like the sound of it. His face twisted, but that was all he had time for. Tice's shot smashed him backward out of the saddle. The spooked horse, snorting, whirled away, stirrups flapping, into the grove of scrub oak. The crew sat like clothes stuffed with straw, never moving.

"If there's anyone else . . . ?" Tice said, pushing his stare at them.

There may have been some who would have liked to quit but none of them was foolish enough to admit it.

"All right," Tice said, sliding his gun back in leather. "We dunno about Jo but we damn sure know where Brett sent Trone's sister. That's where we'll come up with him. Let's git whackin'."

RHODE Island Red was too taken up with the stimulating views he was putting across the slide of his mind to have much attention left over for actualities. In these fantasies the raw damp of wind-cuffed rain, puddled earth and sopping clothes had no existence. The kid, in these dreams, had a sultan's power, time stood still, his slightest whim was law. It made him swear with a kind of balked savagery to find himself still astride a spraddle-legged horse that was stopped head-down before the Red Wall's tie rack.

How long he'd been sitting there like a nump for all to stare at Red didn't know, but the rain had quit—at least for the moment, and a blur of peering faces hurriedly withdrew from his inspection as his glance swept around.

He got out of the saddle and pulled the stuck cloth away from his crotch and the numbed cheeks of his bottom. Dark, sullen clouds, low and turgid with moisture, hung scarcely a rope's throw above the false fronts of the town's drenched buildings. The monotonous drip from nearby eaves was a continuing irritant falling into catch barrels and tock-tocking where others should have stood on warped and splintery planking. Pooled water filled every hollow of the wheel-gashed road, unpleasantly reminding Red of the rankness of his surroundings. A sudden chill made him shiver and he tugged the limp brim of his sopping felt, glaring fiercely, alone in a town whose overwhelming hostility would have taken care of him long ago if its denizens had had half the guts of a tame rabbit.

He sneered, hitching his belt up, and wrung a twist of discolored water from his coat. His glance passed again over the patched-up rigs and spavined horses dejectedly standing in this rain-rankened muck. The holy Joes were in town, that raggedypants scrabble of two-bit owners Tice was going to run out of the country. Ought to be a laugh or two there while he waited; he was sure Lola hadn't come in yet.

He went up on the porch in his muddy boots. Roughly shouldering the batwings he pushed inside. They were here all right— the whole stinking bunch of them, packed solid along the bar. He singled out Bud Lahr, the loudest mouth among them, and with a lift of anticipation started toward him across the floor.

Like the run of wind through a field of grain a clotting silence quickly swept the room around Lahr, getting through to him finally. He quit waving his arms, stiffened and turned as the clomp of Red's boots came over the floor. Lahr's eyes, finding the kid, sprang wide, his cheeks blanching.

Red grinned. "So you think it's time for a change do you, Lahr? What's the matter?" he asked, enjoying the man's consternation. "Can't find your tongue? Why I heard it was big as a muley cow's. Here," he said, reaching out, "let me help you."

The cowman attempted nervously to dodge as men on both sides fell wildly scrambling away, but the bar was too near and Lahr was jammed up against it, pinned there by Red's throttling grip.

Physically the kid was no match for the rancher; every

shocked watcher in the place was aware of this. They knew also why Lahr, gray-faced and sweating, just hung there and took it; he was afraid to fight back, remembering the fellows Red had killed —afraid of doing anything which might tend to set off the kid's retributive temper.

Red, sensing this, reveled in it. He felt ten feet tall, ready and willing to take them all on. "Open up," he growled, "I'm goin' to find that tongue." When Lahr opened his mouth the kid snorted. "Looks big enough to me! You got horses, Lahr—know what a jaw cord is?"

Lahr, aghast, shakily nodded, not trusting his voice. It was inconceivable this young blackguard meant. . . . But he did; Lahr could see it in those jeering eyes, in the hateful grin that was peeling Red's lips back. "Get the apron there to hunt up a piece of twine for you— Tell him right now," the kid said, letting go of Lahr, shoving him.

The rancher, staggering, caught himself, swept a despairing glance over that sea of locked faces, finding no eye that would meet his own. He couldn't blame them honestly but did just the same, knowing that if they'd speak up for him now there was a chance the kid wouldn't do this.

"You goin' to speak your piece?" The kid looked ugly.

Abandoning his pride Lahr stumbled through it.

"That's no way to ask a favor," Red declared. "You want to explain the situation, put a little life in it. Do it like this. Say 'Mister Red here has got a little experiment he wants to try; he wants to hitch up a man the way a Injun does his horse—that's so if there's any bucking he'll be able to control it. I'd like a piece of twine if you got some; couple of yards would be about right.' " Red grinned at Lahr. "You got that?"

Lahr couldn't move. He couldn't open his mouth even. "Say it!"

Lahr's mouth worked but nothing came out.

"By God if you don't I'll ride you all over town!"

The barkeep, thinking to help Lahr, said, "I ain't got no twine, Red—"

"You want some of this, too?" The kid didn't give the man time to answer; he'd got hold of a crueler notion. "Get a rope off one of those horses outside."

Lahr almost retched he was so shaken. The barkeep, pasty cheeks averted, went out. No one else moved with this ugliness loose in the room mocking all of them. None of this crowd looked at Lahr or allowed their eyes to stray toward Red. Each clearly felt the weight on his conscience and was galled by it, humiliated, yet bitterly careful to give no cause for involvement. They had their own lives and families to think about.

Red laughed, openly taunting them. Some of them looked a little apoplectic but nobody did anything.

The barkeep came back with the rope but the kid waved him away. "Lahr's job," he grinned. "Toss him a knife to cut it up with."

When Lahr wouldn't take the rope the apron let go of it, the coils clattering on the floor. He dropped a pocketknife beside it.

The ugly silence crept back.

"Pick 'em up," Red said.

The cowman's cheeks were glistening with sweat and the backs of his shaking hands were beaded with it.

"Pick 'em up!"

Lahr's bones creaked almost audibly as he bent but he wouldn't reach out. He wouldn't touch the rope or pick up the knife. He had both hands against the floor like crutches and hunkered there, glaring up at the kid with the fanatic look of a man who would sooner die than go farther. And he plainly expected Red to kill him.

This wasn't what Red had expected at all. It amounted to defiance and the kid, alone in this place with the bunch of them, suddenly got a different view of the whole proceedings. Somehow the shoe had got on the wrong foot and all the fun was gone out of this. He didn't like what he saw in all those watching eyes.

He ought to drop that son of a bitch right now before this got out of hand, but he knew if he started a move toward his gun these two-bitters would tear him to pieces—it was in their faces, in the way they were eying him—daring him almost.

The hoofs of a horse walked across the stillness, traveling west in the slop outside, moving along the Red Wall's front. The kid struck his forehead with the flat of a hand, giving a good ham performance of a man tardily recalling a forgotten importance, the urgence of which became too plain to doubt. He spun in a lumbering run for the doors, shoving men out of his way, swearing at those who didn't move fast enough. It was a distraction—what he needed, swerving their attention. That it might also presently whet their curiosity—him quitting the place on the heels of that horse, perhaps even to the point of sending them after him, was a chance he had no way of avoiding. Anything was better than what he'd seen shaping up.

Red wanted out, and got out; and damn good thing he'd come out when he had, because the rider passing through the lights of those windows was Lola Trone.

Something—perhaps the intensity of his glance or the sound dragged up off the boards by his rowels—twisted her shoulders around and she saw him, recognition altering all the lines of her face.

"Hey—wait!" Red called, but she put spurs to her horse, kicking him into a run.

Red looking after her suddenly grinned. She wouldn't get far on that hide! Cutting a glance over the tethered broncs standing round him he jerked loose a set of reins and, vaulting up, kicked out with his own spurs. If he contrived to do nothing else he simply had to keep her out of the lights, drive her into the dark where her sex, unseen, would not bring down on him the piled-up wrath of too many bitter memories, too many humiliations sprung from things Hobbled O had done. Crowd her into the dark and then, if he caught her, finish one job to his completest satisfaction. "If, *hell!*" he said, and put the steel to his horse.

BRETT, riding through the day's lingering grayness, was as whipped down and gloomy as he'd ever felt. He could not shake the feeling that had settled so heavily on him when he'd seen his sister die. It was one thing to break her hold on this country, something entirely different to see her killed and know himself responsible. Mora's bullet, sure—but meant for Brett. No way to shift the blame. If he hadn't come back she would still be alive; if he'd stayed away from the ranch she'd be alive; that was what it boiled down to. It made no difference that Tice and her crew had left him no choice, that they'd driven him here. He'd intended ever since he'd got up to come over; had been prepared, should nothing else serve, to burn her out. Well, she was gone, never again to impose her will. The buildings were gutted—he'd had to do that, had to cut Tice off from his base of operations. Only by driving him into the open could Brett show Tice's true stripe, cut him clear of Hobbled O.

And this wasn't done yet. More blood would flow. More men would die. Blood and death—they were like a curse latched onto him. Like that bird hung round the Mariner's neck!

God, but he was sick of it! It was a taste in his mouth, bitterest of all because he knew he wasn't done with it and likely never would be. What he'd started with fists would be finished with guns; nothing else was left in the cards. Nothing else would resolve the black hell stirred here.

His was the fault, and yet—perhaps some good might eventually come of this. As Lola had said that first day, the drought would have finished these people anyway. Things would grow again. Grass would come up and grain would sprout from the bounteous earth this rain had washed; but another year would have to go into it, and these people were in too deep to hang on. Only the holder of their paper. . . .

Great Christ!

Brett, jerked up stiffly, saw the lights of town. In his present turmoil these held little significance; night had overtaken him. *Maybe these folks could be saved at that.* Saved in spite of themselves! That storekeeper, Able, had some of their paper, but it was Hobbled O that had the stranglehold on them and Able, Brett suspected, had been staked by Jo. With Jo gone Brett was Hobbled O—if he could stay alive long enough to prove it. Hell's great Half Acre! He could break the spread up! He could sell off hunks of it— *give* it away! Maybe not back to the outfits Jo'd wiped out, but he could sure take care of the ones still left—he could insure these people's future.

He cautiously felt the bloody rags he'd tied round him; they were still getting the job done. His mind wasn't playing him too fast and loose or he'd be figuring like enough that he might still come through this bullet go-round; he knew better than to munch on any such pap with Tice still about and those Hobbled O hard-cases setting up to take any order he might give 'em. He couldn't stop Tice alone—not even with a gun; he'd never catch Bill Tice alone. But there was other ways he could fix Bill's clock. Judge Temple, if he had to, could bring in deputy U.S. Marshals to clear armed interlopers off an heir's inheritance. Brett slapped his leg. By God, he'd do it; show him how he wanted the place parceled out!

There'd be just about time.

Brett was under no illusion that Tice had given up. Tice had to force this to a finish. It was the chance of a lifetime for a feller like Bill—how else would he ever latch onto such a spread? The crew—at least the men with him, were undoubtedly hand-picked. These would do what he told them to, being what they were; and he would know by now that Jo was dead. The rest of this sequence was tailor-made for him. Kill the heir and have his inheritance! And Brett's own acts were all the cover Tice needed. Brett was a troublemaker. Brett had killed Jo. Vengeance was the only course left for Jo's range boss. Tice would appreciate this. Tice would love it.

So would that kid.

SYD Stoker, the marshal, pulled into town just a few minutes after Rhode Island Red had made his headlong departure from the Red Wall; some of the greasy-sackers were still standing on its porch peering off through the night in the direction of Old Town. Stoker looked too and didn't see a thing. "Something up?"

The small-spread owners swapped glances. Bud Lahr, looking a little queer about the gills, shook his head.

Stoker said, "I'm goin' to try to see that you boys get some help."

That pulled their eyes around. But Stoker didn't see no leap of hope in them. About all he saw was skepticism and suspicion; they were wondering what chestnut he was reaching for now.

The marshal looked at them levelly. "It's Tice who'll be movin' you out of here; Jo—Hobbled O—will be back of it of course, but Tice'll do the dirty work. Now—"

"You ain't sellin' me any part of this," Lahr said.

Several of the men around Lahr nodded. One of these, scowling, stared again toward the river, lost down there in the dark among the ruins of the original settlement. "You been packin' Jo's star for six years, Stoker—"

"I know it. I done wrong—been thinkin' wrong, just like the rest of you. Takin' the easy way, puttin' up with things I knowed warn't right, shiftin' and dodgin' to hang onto what little I've got." The marshal said more firmly, "Brett Fasken's showed me somethin'; he's showed me that outfit ain't as tough as we've reckoned."

"Talk's cheap," Lahr said, but there was a different look about

Stoker, they all saw it; the man stood straighter, carried his head like half his age had dropped away. Spoke different, too. But Stoker hadn't been down on the floor the way Bud just had with a snake like that kid standing over him, taunting him. That ghastly experience would probably stick in Bud's mind for the rest of his days; it made this new hold on life doubly precious to Lahr, and he said bitterly, "Listenin' to you is like to git a man killed plumb dead."

Stoker said, studying them, "There's risk in everything—some damn skylarkin' ranch cook might run you down just crossin' the street. You might git killed by a critter tailin' her out of a bog. Life's full of chance. It's full of hell too, but if you will do what I tell you it might just be you'll git to stick it out here. Jo can't do much without Tice backin' her. I propose to take care of Tice."

"Take care of—" Lahr stopped with his mouth open. The whole push eyed Stoker like he'd cut loose for the moon.

He grinned dryly. "I know it ain't hardly to be thought of, but Tice is just one man—"

"He's got a damn rough crew behind him!"

"Cut off the head an' the rest will quit wrigglin'."

"An' who's goin' to cut it off?" Lahr said belligerently.

"All of us," Stoker said. "I'll handle the cuttin' if you boys'll stand back of me."

"An' if somethin' comes loose," one of Lahr's friends growled, "he'll hunt down every damn fool was in on it!"

"He's goin' to hunt you down anyway. Be after you right now if he wasn't tryin' to plant Fasken. He'll get around to you."

There wasn't any answer to that and they knew it.

The report of a gun came hollowly up from the river. Twice more flat cracks of sound slapped up out of the dark. "Come on," Stoker said, "I'll swear in the bunch of you." He reached for his reins. No one else moved a whisker.

Lahr spoke for all of them. "We ain't liftin' a finger for that damn Brett Fasken! If that's him and Tice bustin' loose down

there leave 'em at it; mebbe they'll both kick. If Tice shows here—
if he comes skallyhootin' in with them Hobbled O sons a bitches,
we'll see you get every chance you got comin'. That's as far as
we'll go. An' if that kid's along with 'em we want him got too."

BRETT didn't push the tired horse; he was trying to keep
something left in him for when Tice and his gun-wavers came
shoving up off his back trail. He reckoned it wouldn't be long—
the man knew this range like the palm of his hand. All Brett
had built on was enough time to reach the judge, to make everything Tice had done go for nothing. That would hurt Bill worse
than any bullet.

He'd done a lot of uncomfortable thinking about Lola, remembering the hope he had opened up for her. He couldn't take
back any part of that. This was going to be bad for her but he
didn't have to make it worse. He meant to stay clear away from
her. He saw no chance of coming through; had given up any hope
of this the moment he'd seen Trone's riddled body. Trone had
been nothing, a straw man, a whipping boy; his misfortune was
simply that he'd been too handy. Brett—in Tice's book—was dangerous. The clean break was best. Sometime, maybe, Lola would
get over it.

Brett didn't much like that thought either.

Coming into the west end of town he tried to recall where
he'd seen the judge's shingle. Hadn't been right in the heart of
things—more off east a ways, seemed like.

It was then he caught the flog of hoofs back of him; not loud
at first, more a mutter but steady like a long roll of drumsticks,
growing, sweeping nearer, raising a track of cold flesh along his
back.

He was half turned, listening, trying to gauge how much time
he had, when two sharper sounds like dry sticks snapping bounded
out of the dark lower reaches of the river.

There are moments when all one's faculties appear literally to freeze under the impact of knowledge. Lola came instantly into Brett's head. He didn't try to explain it. He put the horse down the bank that fell off the right, seeing the huddle of gun-clutching figures milling in front of the Red Wall, not even thinking about them, putting all of his strength into keeping the horse's head up, feeling him squat—hoping to hell he could see in this blackness. Shale rolled under them, mud and clay twisted; once the horse ducked a branch that damn near tore Brett out of the saddle. And then he remembered the kid, the try Red had made at Trone's ranch to get hold of her; and his mind had room for just one desire.

He came onto another curl of road, crossed it; the horse, fighting his head, frantically striving to cut away from that blacker dark which was all that was visible beyond the far edge. Brett, though his dug-up memory of this place had several holes eaten out of it, remembered the stretch as dangerous, the slope—sandstone-pierced in a number of jagged outcrops—dizzily dropping in its rush for the bottoms. It had one advantage: It would get a man down there quicker than he could say *Popocatepetl*.

He used the bit cruelly, forcing the panicked horse to come around, hearing scared yells, the racket of rifles; scarcely aware of this. It was those isolated shots exploded out of the black below which had all of his bitterest attention. If that were Lola down there—and he was convinced it was, it must have been her that had been doing the shooting. No man—even Red—would hardly fire at a woman. It must have been Lola trying to stand the kid off with her pistol.

Had she done it? Had she run out of shells? Had Red reached her while the piece was unloaded?

Brett dug the horse with his gut hooks. They went over the lip, straight out into space. It was like nothing Brett had ever experienced; the horse squealing, terrified, air whistling round them—dropping, wildly plummeting, the roar of the river, everything inside him squeezed and quaking against his teeth. A bullet, Brett thought, would have been merciful beside this.

He was trying to make himself limp when they struck like a dropped wagon. The horse went out from under, screaming. Brett, jackknifed, breathless, hurtled through the dank air like something flung from a catapult. He went thirty feet through mud on his belly, still gripping Trone's sixshooter, not knowing for sure if this were hell or the other place. His belt caught on the exposed root of a cottonwood and he was jerked half around, the last of his breath jolted out of him.

Even after he found he was breathing he made no effort to move, to disentangle himself. Like a sack of burst yams he stayed huddled there numbly, not aware that he was scared to find out if he were hurt. He seemed to be neither awake nor wholly asleep, content to leave everything just as it was.

The wink of muzzle flash, the hard slap of a bullet plowing into congealed earth about an arm's length away, jarred him back to reality—shock breaking through shock. It pushed him onto a knee, discovering his fist still wrapped about Trone's gun.

Things began to come back, to shape up in his mind. When the fellow tried again, firing blindly, Brett judged him cached somewhere in the vicinity of Butterfield's old station—a relic, in Brett's mind, of happier days. He had no idea where Lola was but she would probably be close, too close to risk chucking lead around promiscuous.

He began to crawl nearer, still gripping Trone's gun. How much use it would be to him Brett didn't know; he didn't waste any thought on this. The next sight of muzzle flame showed by its angle that the man had changed position.

Several minutes dragged by without further sound. Brett, flat against soggy ground, made out the breached lift of what was left of the walls, a more solid dark against the night's drifting blackness. The sullen growl of the river, running bank to bank, drowned most of the noises, leaving only the raucous croaking of frogs and the occasional scraping thud of some uprooted debris tearing past rock.

Brett tried to picture the station from memory. Most of the details were fuzzy; all he could be sure of was the fellow was out there waiting for Brett to give him a target.

Why not? Brett thought; but then another thought stayed him, the picture of Lola hiding there someplace. He couldn't risk the unpredictable, the possibility that, firing into the fellow's muzzle wink, he might just plain miss or be thrown off aim. He started forward again, slithering laboriously along on his belly, gaining ground slowly.

Sweat bound the shirt across his shoulders like a plaster. Dank bits of dead weed shook down his open collar, and several times he got into stinging patches of sand burrs. But he kept doggedly on, the squish and scrape of his progress lost in the voice of the river.

He'd heard gunfire above, but it was all stopped now.

It was blacker down here than a hill of stacked stove lids and it was on Brett's mind he might unwittingly come up on the girl and touch off a scream or—worse—catch a bullet intended for the kid. But there was no help for it; he had to get nearer to help her, for if he fired at all that one shot had to do it. There was very little likelihood he'd get a second chance.

Using his forearms, dragging himself forward, he came within twenty feet of where the gun had last spoken without spotting Red. Each abused muscle ached like a rotten tooth and there was a crick in his thigh. In the midst of these tribulations his left outstretched arm with all the weight of both shoulders came down on a broken-off prickly pear pad; he had to grind his jaws against the leaping pain of it. He lay there shaking for what seemed ages before he could scrape up the strength to pry it loose with the barrel of Trone's sixshooter.

The station's nearest eroded wall, some four foot high by his best judgment, rose just ahead. Brett kept on until he could touch it.

He had all his screwed-tight senses pushed out ahead of him like the feelers on a beetle. He couldn't hear a thing above the sound of tumbling water and the frogs' renewed palaver. He could see even less in this dark but every instinct warned him there was somebody crouched just beyond that wall.

Pulling off the limp-brimmed wreck of his hat, bunching the soggy felt in one fist and using the other—which held Trone's tipped-up pistol—to steady him, Brett eased off the ground with a kind of taut care and, praying the barrel of Trone's gun wasn't clogged, extended the hat gingerly over the wall and let go of it.

Lola's scream sheered up like the lunge of a rattler. Red fired, the blast of his piece not ten feet away from where Brett hugged the wall, the slap of its strike stinging his face with adobe, Brett's own weapon racketing right on the heels of it.

Something staggered in the blackness off to the left. A choked curse that was more than half sob came out of it. Something fell and for eerie moments made a kind of wild thrashing while Brett held his fire; and then the river sounds covered it and Lola cried, "Brett! Brett—where are you?"

"Right here," Brett said.

He found her hand, astonished at the coldness of her fingers, the shaking fierceness of their grip. Been more scared than she'd let on, he reckoned. He growled, "Red's gone," in a gruff attempt to comfort her, and was completely confused—even turned a little indignant and angry, at the sudden way she twisted free and stepped back from him.

"Oh, you fool!" she cried. "Bill Tice isn't gone!"

"Well, no," Brett said, "but—"

"He'll hunt you down if it's the last thing he does! Do you think he— Oh, Brett! Let him have the ranch. There are other places. We can start. . . ."

Brett was shaking his head. She was beside herself, not thinking straight, half out of her mind with what she'd been through. He could feel the fear in her and tried to get past it: "You wouldn't want a man who saved his hide at the expense of his self-respect. Pride is all I've got left, Lola."

"I don't want you dead!"

There it was—what he'd sensed this would come to from the night at Scab 8 when they'd swept everything aside. Now she was facing what he'd foreseen she'd likely have to, the emptiness and heartbreak. . . .

"Brett, you don't have to prove—" She clutched his arms, her eyes imploring him; he didn't have to see to understand. It was in her voice, in her frightened grip—the torture of all those intolerable tomorrows.

He said, well knowing the richness of all she was offering, "There are some things a man has to do. I've got to go back." He took hold of her elbows. "If Tice is up there I'll have to face him."

"And if he's not you'll go?"

"I'll still have to face him. I'll have to stay until I do."

She had more fiber than he'd guessed. She stepped back, still eying him. She'd made her try and failed but there were no recriminations. "Of course," she said, and took his arm. "But don't think you're going up there alone."

THEY took the long way around, going up by the road. Walking because they couldn't find Red's horse and Red had killed Lola's, and Brett's, when they discovered him, had to be shot. As they picked their way through the ghostly damp past the moldering ruins of the original town, Brett roughed in what he proposed to do about Hobbled O and the crew of toughs Tice had gathered about him. Even if they returned the acreage Jo had forcibly seized they would still have a pretty fair spread; and they would have Scab 8.

But he knew her mind wasn't on land or cattle. Too clearly she saw what lay ahead, and no amount of conversation was going to sweeten the prospect. Brett quit trying and somberly strode beside her, largely filled with the same frustrations.

Gloom hemmed him in. His own bull stubbornness had triggered this trap; he wouldn't run when he could and now he couldn't—not and continue to live with himself. He was bound to face Tice.

He didn't see how he could lick this deal; the most he could hope for was to cut Tice down. But there again Tice would have the advantage. His bunch would have rifles, Brett's Winchester was still with his horse. All he had was Trone's belt gun with three cartridges in it.

He was about to search his pockets for those Lola had gotten him when a clatter sounded from the dark loop of road above. For seconds the sound hung suspended in isolation. Something then crashed against the slope with a ripped-up mutter of broken branches. Rubble commenced to slip up there, gathering sound like a full-scale slide.

Lola pulled at Brett nervously. In this terrifying murk he couldn't be sure which direction was safest, and while they stood rooted a startled curse lifted out of the blackness ahead. Brett shoved Lola flat in the mud.

Tice's bull-throated roar leaped out of the night. "You're cut off, Fasken! Throw down your guns!"

Brett knew better than to give Tice anything to target his gun on.

"Strike a match!" Tice snarled. "I'm countin' three. If you ain't showed—"

"You got down to shootin' up women, have you? I should of thought gunning Jo would've been enough for you."

Tice didn't care for that remark none whatever. He was not so secure in his control of this deal he could afford to have talk of that kind going around. He said, trying to make them out through the gloom, "You got that Trone filly with you?" and when the stillness ran on with no sound but the river: "Give her a match an' she can light up an' go."

"And what happens to him?" Lola cried.

"He gets an escort outa the country."

Brett grinned in the dark. Any escort he got from Bill Tice would be a bullet. Lola must have suspected this too, for she said, "Let me talk to the marshal."

"Stoker's dead. Now you listen to me," Tice shouted. "I got this town eatin' outa my hand. That hardscrabble bunch of greasy-sackers is gone—Flagler's gone too." He stopped to let that sink in. "I ought to give you billy-hell, burnin' that place out! Bein's you ain't got a leg to stand on I'm lettin' you go—both of you, but by God I aim to *see you doin' it!* Strike a light!"

Tice got his light from an unexpected quarter. A bundle of oil-soaked rags came bounding and blazing off the dark road above. Several others came swiftly after it and in this flare Tice's crew stood out like gobs of corn on a Christmas tree. Spread across the road and along both sides with their weapons held ready to cut loose on cue, the weird illumination avalanching toward them down the slope unsettled them as badly as would a herd of charging elephants—it was just about as incredible.

Into this confusion of squealing pitching horses, shouting riders and the wild cursing of Tice, slugs began to batter and whine from the rosettes of muzzle flame dotting the rim. Three of Tice's crew went headlong out of their saddles. Two horses went down. Apparently the cowed townsmen and maybe some of the despised two-bitters were not as whipped as Tice had thought. One Hobbled O hardcase, unhorsed, frantically scuttling for cover, was knocked sprawling before he had taken two jumps.

This much Brett saw before a blow like the scrape from a piece of bar iron, half tearing his belt off, spun him around to face Tice coming at him full gallop. The man had a gun in each fist, and was firing as fast as he could trip his hammers. The whine of that lead was all about Brett and he was practically staring into the horse's distended nostrils—in imminent peril of being run down—when he tipped up Trone's gun.

The horse veered away from the muzzle flash. Tice, jaws wide in a terrible cry, went heels over head, striking heavily. Brett, not knowing if he was going to be able to hold onto his grub, was turning away to look for Lola when Tice got an elbow under him and fired.

The shock of impact drove Brett backward. His legs couldn't seem to get any purchase. Everything about him appeared to spin with dizzying violence. He had no recollection of blacking out but the next thing he knew the road was bright with gleaming lanterns and he was down on his back staring into a million faces. Well—not quite a million maybe, but they must have included the entire town and a couple of pretty fair handfuls off the outlying ranges.

There was Fletcher and Flarity and the Packer's Crossing barber and old Judge Temple and Bud Lahr and his Missus and two-three dozen others he couldn't right handy hitch names to—and the damndest thing about the whole deal was every one of them bastards was grinning. It was enough to make a feller think he'd slipped his pin or woke up in a looney house!

They even by God had a bandage on him, and the way they was crowding and reaching it looked like every cockeyed one of them was fixing to wring his flipper!

He said, rolling his eyes around, "What happened to Tice?" and the way it come out he looked up quick to see who had said it, not believing his voice could act that way; and not too many appeared to have heard but those that did began pounding each other like he'd cut a real shine.

Then the judge was shooing them back. "Just lay quiet, son, you got him. You given this country a new lease on life and ain't none of these boys that's goin' to forget it."

Lola was saying, "Judge, when can we move him?" and Brett, twisting somewhat, found she had his head in her lap, sitting right here in all that damn wet! He let her push him back but got hold of her hand. He was looking ahead now, forgetting the past—and finding it uncommon queer to be doing so. But he knew what he wanted. "Ain't about to go nowhere," he grumbled, "till some body gets me an' this filly hitched—"

"You *been* hitched," the judge said. "Great sakes, don't you remember!"

Date Due